TIGER TRACKS

ALASKAN TIGERS: BOOK NINE

MARISSA DOBSON

Dedication

To my readers, who have loved the Alaskan Tigers series as much as I do. Styx has always been one of my favorites. He's still coming to terms with his past and his future has many twists and turns. There's still so much more to his story than just this book.

To my husband, who took Pup Cameron out of my office and played with him when I needed to work. For Pup Cameron who eventually realized Mommy couldn't play all the time.

To my amazing team. Teresa Riley, Rosa Sophia, Brynna Curry, and Allyson Brann. Each of you are amazing. Thank you for all your hard work.

Finally to my street team, Marissa's Dreamweavers, you are all marvelous. I hope you enjoy Styx and Mira's story.

Chapter One

At thirty-thousand feet in the air, Styx rose to his feet and searched the maps of Washington D.C., doing his best to get a firm idea of the city before they landed. Somehow, in a city of over a half a million residents and countless others who traveled into the city for work, he was supposed to find one tigress who was on the run with a bounty on her head. Easy, right? He doubted it.

They weren't even sure if she was still there. One lone transmission to the shifter forum was all they had to go on. Trey, one of the Kodiak Bears, had traced the origin of the message, so that was their starting point. He hoped that even in the midst of all the people here, he'd be able to catch the scent of the tigress. If not, it was going to make his job even harder.

Turbulence bounced the plane, sending him sidestepping until he grabbed hold of a table to keep himself upright. His stomach rolled and he swore if he looked in a mirror, he'd have a green tinge to his skin. "Damn it, Theodore, keep this damn plane still."

"Is the big tiger scared of a little turbulence?" The youngest of the Brown brothers, Theodore, called out from the cockpit with a chuckle.

"You're the one who put me back here surrounded by this furniture. The idea of turbulence shaking this stuff loose and falling on me isn't my idea of a fun night." He tried to hide the fact he hated to fly. Being shoved in a tin box with wings as they flew thousands of miles in the air had never given him comfort. If the ride was smooth, he was able to keep it out of his mind, but add in some bumps and there was no way he'd forget they could fall out of the sky with little warning.

"We'll do what we have to in D.C.," Theodore said. "Then we'll take this to Jinx and Summer in West Virginia. After that, you'll have the rest of the plane to yourself. Well, unless we find that tigress ourselves."

"There's no *unless*. We'll find her and get her somewhere safe." More turbulence rocked the plane, sending Styx two steps to the right before he was able to gain control. "Less chit-chat and more flying," he bitched through gritted teeth.

He tried to turn his attention back to the maps before him, but it was no use. There was nothing new on them, no clue as to where the tigress would have gone. Maps didn't tell him where he'd go if he were in her shoes. Only being there, getting into her mindset, would do that. He had spent many years tracking down shifters, years he'd rather not remember. He'd do it again, but this time for a good cause. There would be no blood or death, at least he hoped not, and if there were, then it wouldn't be him causing it.

He knew what others thought of him—a ruthless assassin—but he had only done what he was ordered to do. He wasn't proud of it, but he had made the world a little safer by eliminating those who were a danger to others. Now, as the second in command of the guards for Bethany—the mate of the Alaskan Tigers' Lieutenant—he was making up for the nasty things he did in his past.

Working with Shadow—the Captain of Bethany's Guards—and Bethany had brought out a better part of him. He wanted to do more than just kill to keep their world safe. He wanted to find the same kind of love Bethany and Raja shared.

All the years he had been traveling on missions, he had never found the *one*, and some days he wondered if he ever would. Maybe due to his crimes against others in his past, he would be punished. Maybe he would never find his mate.

Turbulence once again rocked the plane from side to side, sending him toward the row of seats. "I'm going to end up with two broken legs if you keep this up."

"Take a seat, it's going to get rough," Theodore hollered, but Styx had already plopped down on the only row of seats in the plane and begun to buckle himself in.

With an unsupportive tiger clan in D.C., there was a good chance they'd run into some enemies as he searched for the tigress, so he needed to be in top form. That meant no broken bones from Theodore's flying. He let his head fall back against the stiff seat and tried to get into the tigress's mind. He wanted to keep the trip to the capitol as short as possible. Less time equaled less of a chance to run into any of the clan members who had been sent out to hunt the tigress.

The Washington D.C. Tigers might be one of the smallest clans to hold out on committing to Tabitha as Queen of the Tigers, but that didn't make them any less of a threat. The Washington D.C. Tigers were made up of mostly men. Some would consider them a group of tigers no other clan wanted. For a moment, he wondered if he would've joined them if the Alaskan Tigers hadn't taken him in. Most of the Washington D.C. Tigers had an extensive history of causing problems with other clans and even humans. It made sense to Styx that he might've gotten stuck with them. He considered himself lucky.

Tabitha's rule over all tigers would put a stop to this sort of thing. They might hold out now, but eventually they'd be seen as too big of a threat to be left alone. The only reason they hadn't been considered a high risk yet was because of Randolph and his gang of rogue shifters. One day, it would be safe for all tigers under Tabitha's rule, and eventually all shifters. They'd see to it.

No matter the danger, he was proud to be a part of it. It not only gave him a chance to make up for his past, but it would make their world a safer place once Tabitha had completed the prophecies. Future shifter generations would grow up in a world that accepted their species. They'd no longer have to worry about being hunted down, or having to keep their secret hidden. One day, shifters and humans would live side by side in harmony. At least, they could hope.

He longed to see that day. Though, knowing he played a part in it made all the difference to him. It didn't matter that his part was small. It only mattered he was making up for his sins by changing the world into a more positive place for future generations of tigers. The future was what mattered, and Tabitha still had a lot left to do before the prophecies were complete.

He glanced out the window just as the first specks of lights from D.C. were beginning to shine through the clouds. They were like diamonds in the dark, reminding him just how big the city was. This was going to be like finding a needle in a haystack. One tigress in a herd of people was going to be nearly impossible.

Find her scent. It will lead you right to her, he reminded himself. It wasn't like he hadn't done this before. He had been chosen for this mission because of his past. If anyone could find her, it was him. He wasn't just known among his kind for being an assassin, but also for being the best tracker. It had been a while since he'd done this type of work, but one never forgets. It was like shifting. The knowledge was still there.

"We'll be landing in a few, and there's an SUV standing by for us, so figure out where you want to head," Theodore called back to him as the plane started its decent.

"We'll go to the transmission location and start there." One question remained unanswered. What was she doing in Foggy Bottom? Was it special to her? Or was she sticking close to the tourists, trying to blend in? The metro area would have been busy, and there'd have been plenty of places to hide there, even at the time of night she'd sent her cry for help.

She must have figured it would be harder to find her and kill her in D.C. because of all the people, but by going there, she was also putting civilians as risk. It made the situation that much more urgent. If the hit man from her clan found her, others could get caught in the middle. It was a mess they'd have a hard time cleaning up, especially if any of them shifted. The government didn't know their species existed, and that's how they wanted to keep it. *For now.*

When the plane came to a stop on the runway, he shot up, and gathered the maps and papers that he had laid out on one of the tables. Desperate to get out of this tin box, he shoved everything in his bag.

"Stop lumbering around back there and give me a minute to shut her down. I want to fill her up with gas as well before we leave, in case we have to leave in a hurry."

Styx stifled a growl. He was anxious to begin the search. Waiting a few extra minutes while the plane was prepared for their return flight wouldn't make much of a difference now, especially if it could save their lives if things went downhill later.

"I've got to check my phone, and I'll warm up the SUV," he replied. *Anything to get off this damn thing.* He slung the bag over his shoulder and headed for the exit, just as the engines shut down. He tugged the handle and the door opened, giving him a small set of stairs to descend.

At the foot of the steps he paused and let the cool winter air wash over him. Even the freezing temperatures didn't stop him from enjoying the fresh, crisp air. He slipped his phone from his pocket and powered it up. The minute the screen lit up, the phone vibrated in his hand announcing a text message from Ty. *The text at the bottom was a location. Translating now. May take some time.*

A location? He pulled up the transmission that the forum had received from the woman but he still couldn't make heads or tails of the last line.

According to Ty's message, it was some kind of code that would lead them to her location. He stared at the text, but it wasn't any code that he was aware of. Nevertheless, if his Alpha said it was a location, then there was no doubt about it. Hopefully, it would lead them to her, because other than tracking a scent, he had no way to locate her. No description or name. He was truly on a wild goose chase—or maybe that should be *wild tigress chase*. The only thing that might make her scent stand out was fear. If she controlled herself enough to mask that, then he was in dire straits.

Along with the Washington D.C. Tigers, there might be other shifters who had traveled there for vacation, tourism, or just work. Any tigress scent he caught from the location of the transmission might be hers, or it might not be. He could spend the next several hours running down false leads, instead of actually tracking the woman he was after.

He tossed his things into the back and climbed into the driver's seat. His mind worked through the codes that he'd learned as an assassin, but none of them fit with that last line. It just didn't make sense. He'd studied every code that was out there. He might not know them all, but he knew enough about the different ones to recognize something. This was total gibberish. Where did Ty come up with it? It was just another question that was going to have to wait until his Alpha called him. He'd do his job, and when the Elders had information that would help him, they'd contact him.

He glanced at his watch and noticed it was later than he'd thought. The tourists were already tucked in bed at their hotels for the night, or exploring the nightlife the city had to offer, not down in Foggy Bottom helping her stay hidden. *I hope you found somewhere to hide. Stay safe. Help is on the way.*

Darkness had fallen hours before, leaving behind a completely different D.C.

than the one Mira remembered from her visit here years ago. It seemed like every bump in the night held danger, and every passerby seemed more sinister now than hours before. Exhaustion had settled into her muscles long ago, but she forced herself to keep going. Someone would come to help her. If she could just hang on a little longer, she'd get out of this nightmare.

The message she'd sent to the forum would lead them to her. Well, not actually to her, but to a location that would hold another message on how to meet her. She needed to get higher, somewhere that would allow her to observe the bench where she'd left the message. If only she knew when they'd arrive. Her visions couldn't give her useful information like that. All she could see was that help would arrive at that bench sometime when only stars were scattered through the black sky. It might be tonight, or tomorrow, or maybe it wouldn't be for days, but all she could do was wait. There was nowhere she could go. If help didn't arrive, she was on her own, and she wouldn't live long alone.

A man with a tuneless whistle was heading in her direction. He didn't smell like a shifter, but he could be part of a trap. She slinked farther into the alley, hoping to keep her presence a secret. Then she could move on. She fingered the hilt of the knife she'd shoved into the waistband of her jeans. It wouldn't be enough to stop a shifter, but it might give her a chance to escape.

"Hey, darling." The guy was heading directly for her now, his words slurred. He reeked of booze. "Whatya doing…in a place like this? You come home with me. I've got somewhere warm you can stay. I'll give you some of this, and you'll never want to leave." He wiggled his hips, trying to interest her.

He was harmless. Drunk son of a bitch was just looking to get laid, but he was barking up the wrong tree. Even if he didn't reek of booze, and Heaven only knows what else, she didn't have time to get her groove on with some asshole.

"Thanks for the offer, man, but you go on home. I'm waiting for someone."

"He won't be as…good as I am." But the man staggered farther down the alley, leaving her in peace. "You'll miss out on something amazing."

"I've no doubt." To her surprise, she was able to keep the sarcastic tone from her voice. To put distance between her and the drunk, she forced herself from the safety of the alley. She needed to find somewhere else, preferably somewhere where the neighborhood drunks and homeless wouldn't stumble on her and proposition her again. She didn't have the energy to waste on whooping their asses.

She wandered around the city for nearly an hour, waiting for the moon to reach the position she'd seen in her vision. After ensuring no one had followed her, she headed to the lookout point of the night. Each night, she'd have to find somewhere else to watch, but tonight she was going to use the rooftop deck of the hotel. Hopefully, they'd come soon, so she wouldn't have to figure out a place for tomorrow night.

She tucked a strand of hair behind her ear and checked around her once again. Looking over her shoulder was getting old. Even if she could smell a shifter, it didn't mean that her former Alpha wouldn't have sent one of the human members with an assistant to track her movements. The Alpha of the Connecticut Tigers was a vindictive man. He was going to see that she paid for her betrayal. To him, there was no greater sin then a clan member not falling in line with his demands. If she hadn't run, she'd have been tortured for her treachery before he killed her. Her escape bought her time and a quick death if they caught her, but she was hoping for a chance at life.

Please let tonight be the night. Just as someone was leaving the hotel, she came around the corner and caught the door before it could click shut, locking her out. Her timing had been perfect. With a quick glance inside, she didn't see anyone lurking about. She slipped inside and the warmth against her cold skin sent tiny shocks through her as her body began to adjust to the new temperature.

She took her time climbing each step so she could enjoy the warmth for as long as possible before she had to face the cold again. If she could have rented a room without using a credit card, she would have. One with a view of the bench. Hotels, especially nice ones like this one, always wanted credit cards, so she was out of luck. Instead, she was stuck with the roof access. At least this time of year no one would be up there, and if she managed to stay out of sight of the security cameras, she might be able to remain there without getting caught.

She climbed without pause until she reached the roof. There, she waited outside the door and listened. She used her shifter hearing to ensure no one was waiting on the rooftop terrace. Detecting nothing, she pushed the door opened a couple inches and glanced around, while also taking a deep breath of air to see if she could smell if any shifters had been there. Nothing.

She stepped out into the cold. While she moved toward the chest-high railing, she stayed close to the building and out of the range of the camera. She had already scoped out the location earlier in the day, while others were about and she could blend in like the average hotel guest just out to observe the view. She knew the best spot to watch the location while staying out of view of security.

She crept into place and settled in for a long night. She'd stay until the moon had moved on and the sun would be peaking over the horizon, because by then it would be too late for them to come. *If they don't come...*

She tried to push the idea from her thoughts because it would mean another day on her own, scared of her own shadow. She'd never been a fierce tigress, but she wasn't the type to be pushed around, either. Now, everything seemed sinister. Where had her backbone gone?

You had enough backbone to leave your clan. Her inner voice had been with her all her life, and it was the same one she'd heard in her visions. It was comforting. She wasn't alone, even though it felt like she was. The voice returned again, and she relaxed. *You can get through this. Have faith.*

Chapter Two

Due to the late hour, D.C. traffic was light, which was good for Styx as he stood in the middle of the street trying to catch the scent of the tigress. There were so many different smells all demanding his attention. To the left, he could smell a woman who had been there earlier, her strawberry shampoo mixing sweetly with her honey scent. A masculine scent was there as well, overpowered by booze and stress. So far, everything he could smell was human. Where was the tigress? It hadn't been long enough for the trace of her to vanish. A hint of her had to be there somewhere. He let his eyelids fall shut and focused.

Each scent was like a calling card back to their owner, a direct path to them if only he'd follow one. He would follow one if he found the right one, though so far he was having no luck. Then it hit him. It was faint but unmistakable. It wasn't just the fact it was the only tigress scent there, but it was also laced with terror and trace rays of hope. There was something oddly arousing about the scent that had his tiger within sitting up and taking notice.

"Styx." Theodore pulled him from his concentration, making his tiger growl at the interruption.

"Not now."

"It's Ty. He tried your cell but you didn't answer, and he says it's important." He leaned against the side of the SUV, holding out the phone.

He couldn't deny a call from his Alpha even if he wanted to. He might have a translation to the code at the bottom of the tigress's transmission. He

15

took the offered phone and nodded for him to get back into the SUV. As he climbed in himself, he switched on the speaker phone, so Theodore could be updated as well. "I'm here, go ahead. You're on speaker. What do you have for me?"

"The code is being translated, but what we have so far is there's a spot directly across the Potomac River from Arlington Cemetery. Somewhere along the river there will be something waiting for you on a bench."

"That's all you've got?" he snapped, as the excitement of a break shattered. "Do you realize how big that section is or how many benches there will be? It will take hours for us to search them. What about a location for this woman? Anything useful?"

"Tabitha has about half the message translated, but I wanted to get you heading in the right direction first." Ty sighed, and there was a pause. "I'm afraid this won't be the quick trip we were hoping for. Whatever you find waiting on that bench won't be her. It might be another message we'll have to decode. We won't know until you find it."

"There's something else, isn't there?" Styx started up the SUV, kicking on the heat to chase away the chill that hung in the air.

"Jinx received a call." Through the phone, Styx could hear his Alpha moving farther away from the voices that had been in the background. A door clicked shut before he continued. "The Washington D.C. Tigers know there's a shifter in their area. They don't know it's a woman *yet*, but you need to find her and get the hell out of there before shit heads south."

"Fuck!" Theodore cursed, summing up what Styx and everyone else was thinking. They knew it wasn't just the woman who'd be in trouble if the Washington D.C. Tigers learned too much, but *all* of them. Since they hadn't devoted themselves to Tabitha as the Queen of the Tigers, it meant they were as big of an enemy as a group of rouges, only these shifters were a dangerous bunch. Styx and Theodore alone stood no chance again the whole clan.

"Garth and Red are on their way to back up your mission. They'll call when they get to the area. In the meantime, you've got Quinn's cell number. He's in D.C., so call him if you run into any trouble before backup arrives."

Quinn Evans might be local, but there'd have to be a major issue for Styx to call the United States Marshal. The Marshal would demand they play it by the book, and even though Styx's life had straightened out since he had been an assassin, it didn't mean he could play by the book with a woman's life hanging in the balance. He'd go to any lengths to find her and protect her. He'd made mistakes in his past, and it cost him the life of someone he was supposed to protect, but not this time.

"Styx?" Ty's voice held a hint of sadness as if his thoughts were also turning back to Styx's past.

"I'm here." He clipped his phone to the visor so he could talk and drive at the same time without violating the new hands-free driving laws. Police were the last thing they needed, because there was little doubt the local clan had connections there. "We're heading to the location now."

"We'll be in touch when we have the rest of it translated."

"During my…" He searched for the right phrase before finally settling on one. "My…time in the field, I've studied nearly every code. Is this a new one?"

"No. Ancient. We were only able to translate it because of *the book*. When you find her, you're going to need to find out how she knew the code before you can bring her back here. It's so old that it's highly unlikely anyone alive would know it. The only conclusion I can arrive at is that it might've been passed down from generations ago."

The way he said *the book* made it clear that once again Tabitha's special abilities were being utilized. The book was kept in a safe place most of the time, but when she needed it, it was there for her. Other times, when she didn't even realize she needed it, the book would call to her. It had been their map on this journey of uniting all tigers.

"I'll see to it." He reached up to end the call when Ty's voice stopped him.

"It wasn't your fault." The parting words were soft enough that he almost questioned his Alpha had even said them.

"What wasn't?" Theodore glanced at him as they traveled toward their new destination.

"Long story, bear." Scenery flew by as they raced toward the river. "This is more than you signed up for, so I understand if you want to head out." Part of him wanted Theodore to pack it in and go to the West Virginia Tigers. The youngest of the Brown brothers might have seen his fair share of fighting, but he wasn't ready to stand up against the Washington D.C. Tigers if things came to that. And he sure as hell didn't want to have to bring news to the Brown brothers that the youngest was killed.

"You sound like Taber and Thorben. Just because they are the oldest, they feel they know what's best. I've been on missions before, and I'm not backing down. Don't go trying to protect me, because you know my brothers will be pissed if I so much as stub my toe."

Styx couldn't keep the smile off his face. When they got stuck at a traffic light, he glanced across the front seat. "Bear, I only meant this was more than you signed up for. Backup is going to take a while to arrive. We're going to be on our own for at least a couple hours, longer if they drove."

"I'm here until the end. We'll find your tigress, and then all of us can get out of the city and back to the safety of a compound." He tipped his head toward the now green light. "Let's not waste time. Maybe we can find her before they even arrive, and they can turn around."

"Optimistic, but I like it." He was used to working these types of situation on his own. Until he became a part of Bethany's guard, he always worked alone.

Now he was Shadow's second, her right hand man. Shadow had earned her position, even though it was unusual to have a woman as a guard member, not to mention the fact she was still young. Nevertheless, she was fierce and would keep the Lieutenant's mate safe at all costs.

What surprised him was that Shadow had chosen him as her second. He never suspected he'd get a position like this because of his past. Even though the Alaskan Tigers had opened their home and ranks to him, there were still many among his kind who saw him as an assassin and refused to trust him. Even the Lieutenant's sister, Tora, had seen him that way at first. She had only warmed to him after she witnessed his devotion to Bethany, Shadow, and the clan as a whole.

This was another chance to prove that he was more than an assassin, but even that wasn't his priority. It was getting the tigress to safety that was most important. He had earned his reputation as a stone cold killer because of his devotion and skills. It might not be what he wanted to be known for, but it didn't change the fact that people who didn't know him were scared of him. It had benefits. Shifters backed away when they saw him, and that helped keep the Alaskan Tigers' Elders safe. Not just Bethany, but all of them, because it was his duty to protect them. The clan that opened themselves to him was now his family, and he'd die for them. On the flip of the coin, he'd live for them, too. He was fiercely protective of what was his.

Ten minutes later, they pulled up in front of the start of the park area by the Potomac River. The land they had to cover and the number of benches they had to search were numerous but they couldn't separate. Not with the newest threat hanging overhead. They'd have to do this quickly and together. Hopefully, their guess was correct: that she'd have stayed in West Potomac Park instead of heading farther East.

The wind blew, sending the same scent he had smelled at the first location drifting right toward him. This time, his tiger jumped to life, charging forward. He might have doubted that it was the woman he was looking for at the first location, but this time there was no questioning what he smelled. The tigress had been here, weaving in and out of the park. She had looped back so many times it made it hard to know where to start. Each time he thought the path was new and just beginning, the scent leaped around before continuing on. *Paranoid.* But that was understandable with her Alpha's men after her and the Washington D.C. Tigers being a possible danger.

"Don't worry, Catnip, I'm coming for you."

"Huh?" Theodore went to the first bench, checking it over for any signs that she had been there.

"Nothing." He followed the scent around like a puppy dog trying to find his owner. Round and round he went, but his thoughts were on the nickname he had just given her. *Catnip*, because of the way the smell aroused his tiger, bringing the beast forward like a cat searching for a treat. He hadn't even met this woman, and already her smell had his beast on edge.

Just before the slope toward the river, they found the bench. He knew it without even having to look, because that's where her scent was the strongest. She had been there multiple times, most likely checking to make sure whatever message she'd left was still there. His pace quickened as he crossed the park toward the spot.

What would he find there? He already knew he wouldn't find her here, on this bench, but would the next piece of the puzzle lead him to her? Or was it another clue as to where to go next? He had never liked games like this. He'd have rather just hunted her down his own way, instead of skulking around the city, collecting one piece after another.

"Over here." He didn't bother to look back to see if Theodore was coming. Instead, he squatted down next to the bench and felt under the wood planks. There had to be something. He found it taped under the second plank, and he carefully pried it loose and brought it into the light.

He rose and glanced around once again to make sure they were alone in the park. Something had him on edge, almost as if danger was coming their way. He had never had that type of sixth sense before, but his tiger began to pace within him. He trusted his instincts enough to know something was off. His beast was too agitated. It wasn't a false alarm.

"Do you feel that?"

Theodore raised an eyebrow in question. "Man, first you were talking to yourself and now you *feel* something. Are you sure you're okay?"

"You don't feel that tension?" Before the bear could answer, Styx glanced around. "Someone is watching and they're in danger."

"How do you know this? I've seen you in battle before. This isn't a trait of yours. Why the change? Are your powers growing along with Tabitha's?"

"I don't know." He hated to admit it, but he didn't know what was going on. Tabitha and some of the other shifters had noticed changes within them as Tabitha began to grow in power. Everyone was becoming more powerful in order to protect the Queen of the Tigers. However, it was mostly the ones who'd mated that were growing in strength and power. It was as if the book was bringing together mates to make them a more powerful core group. It's what they needed to ensure Tabitha and Ty's safety until they could produce an heir, but it also made their enemies more wary of them.

"It's eerie to watch all of you change as you have," Theodore said. "Not just becoming more deadly and powerful, but there's also some kind of invisible cord connecting all of you. The Elders and their elite guards are acting as if they're one person, of the same mind. It's more than just training together because no matter how much training you have, it's not enough to be able to do what you've done. It's not even just the tigers. I've seen Taber, Thorben, and Tad all become a part of this. It hasn't started with Trey and Turi yet, but Ivy's human, so it might not. She's only connected to your clan through the Kodiak Bears."

He'd have to be blind not to have seen what Theodore was referring to. Over the last several months, he had witnessed it himself. It started slow at first, but recently it had begun to grow intensely. Was it speeding up because the danger level was going to skyrocket soon? He wasn't sure, but he didn't want to spend too much time considering it. "If we're growing, your sleuth will, too. You are an ally, one we cherish. Everything that's happening is for the greater good of our kind. Never doubt that."

"I'm not doubting anything, only stating what I've seen. I don't spend much time at the Alaskan Tigers compound, but I've seen the changes in my brothers when they come to the island. Dad thinks it's because things are going to get dangerous soon."

"How about we focus on one issue at a time?" His cell phone rang, interrupting him just as he had started opening the folded piece of paper in his hand. He unclipped the phone from his belt. The screen read, *Garth*. This time he wouldn't be able to put it on speaker because they were out in the open, but if Theodore listened closely, he'd still be able to hear. "Styx."

"We're just entering the D.C. metro area."

He pulled the phone away from his ear for a moment and glanced at the time. Not enough time had passed for them to drive from Snowshoe, West Virginia. They must have flown, and it would have taken some good connections to get them a vehicle to the airstrip they used outside the city limits on such short notice. Either way, he was relieved to hear backup was on the way. They could separate into two groups and try to determine which direction the tigress headed when she left the park. "We're at West Potomac Park. Head this way, but be on your guard. Something isn't right."

"We're on our way." Garth hung up without another word.

"Just a little longer and we'll have backup." Styx unfolded the paper in his hand. The same coded message he'd seen at the bottom of the first transmission was etched out on the thick white paper.

"How is that supposed to help us?" Theodore plopped down on the bench. "If it takes hours to translate, just like the last one, we'll never find her before the Washington D.C. Tigers know we're here. There are too many of us to go unnoticed for long. Someone will be out and catch our scent."

Styx didn't answer. Instead, he took a snapshot of the paper and messaged it to Ty. They'd work on it, and in the meantime that meant he'd have to figure out which way she went when she left the park. They would head in that direction, following the scent until it was either a dead-end or they found her. Either way, they'd continue while the Elders worked on the code.

Help! A woman's voice screamed at him as if she was right there. He turned, scanning the park, but there was no one around except Theodore who was still seated on the bench, his legs stretched out before him, looking completely unbothered. Had he not heard the woman's cry? He pinched the bridge of his nose and wondered if he was getting too old for missions like this. Obviously, he was hearing things that weren't there, and that didn't bode well.

Someone please...they're coming. The fear that laced those words cut through him like a knife, and terror thickened the air. He had to find her. It could have been her Alpha's men, or the local tigers. Either way, she wouldn't stand a chance if they got to her first.

"Let's go," he ordered Theodore, and jogged toward the entrance of the park. He wasn't heading to the SUV, he was listening to his tiger and following his instincts.

"Where are we going?"

"I know where she is." He couldn't explain how he knew, but she was at the hotel on the far side of the park.

"What? You can read the code now?"

"No, I just know. Hurry up." He broke out into a run. Dashing across the park and toward the hotel in record setting speeds, Theodore kept pace with him until he slid to a halt next to some parked cars across the street from hotel. He shot Garth a quick text message to let them know he was at the hotel instead of the park, and then turned to Theodore. "We go in there and get her out, but I doubt it's going to be easy. Someone is coming or might already be there. I don't know if it's her Alpha's team or the locals. Either way, it could get dicey."

Theodore adjusted the knife that was on his belt, hiding it under his shirt as they made their way through the lobby. They normally carried guns, but they'd decided to leave them in the car since the local clan had a connection with the police. It wouldn't help them if things got bad, but they didn't need the problems that came with carrying illegal weapons. They were playing things as close to the legal limits as they could. However, if things called for it, Styx was more than willing to cross that line to ensure the tigress's safety.

"Let's do this."

Chapter Three

Slowly, they crept toward Mira, and the fear washed through her. She was stuck, with nowhere to hide. They had backed her into a corner. Unless she wanted to jump over the edge of the building, she had nowhere to go. Jump to her death or fall into their hands—she wasn't sure which option was worse. She had been on the far side of the building watching the bench and the two men who had found her message. She had been hoping they were the help she requested. Then, things on the roof had taken a dangerous turn. Not paying attention to her surroundings had cost her.

"We knew there was an unapproved shifter in the area, but we didn't know it would be a woman." The man before her growled. "You're a beauty. We're going to have an unforgettable time with you."

His thick body that seemed to be all muscle was covered with leather from head to toe. His blond hair was pulled back into a ponytail at the base of his skull, but it wasn't his outfit that sent her blood running cold. It was the image of a tiger sewn on the right hand side of the leather jacket. This was a member of the Washington D.C. Tigers. She knew the image would be on the back of his jacket as well; it was their signature. Even though the citizens didn't realize they were shifters, they knew the biker gang was dangerous.

"I don't want any trouble."

As he neared, she pressed herself against the pillar she had been leaning on.

"You should have thought about that before you came into our territory.

Since you're here without protection that makes you ours." He grabbed her wrist and pulled her to her feet.

She wanted to retch as he caressed her face, but she'd bide her time until she saw an opening. With the second guy standing a half dozen feet behind her, this wasn't the time. He'd be on her before she could do any damage to the man before her. Two against one weren't horrible odds, but mix in the little experience she had with physical fighting, and that made for a more dangerous game.

Her Alpha didn't believe in preparing them for what they might face. He only wanted his guards to be able to defend him. After all, when an Alpha was paranoid, his own people seemed like a threat. The best way to combat that is to make sure they're too scared or don't have the ability to fight back.

"I think we should have our way with her and loosen her up before we take her back to the gang." The man behind her stalked forward.

"Lorcan would have us killed for such treason, and this bitch isn't worth my life." He ran his hand down her neck. "We might be able to convince him to give us first go with her if we take her now. Delay and we'll be the last."

"You'd settle on sloppy seconds?" She licked her lips and let her gaze take him in. "Here I thought you were a *real* man." It might have been a bad decision to provoke him, but she'd rather they tried to kill her now than take her to the rest of the clan. If she was going to find her opening to get away, it had to be before they left the hotel. Otherwise, she was dead, or most likely the plaything of their clan before they decided to kill her.

He slammed her against the pillar with enough force that her head bounced off the concrete. If she hadn't been a shifter, she'd have been knocked unconscious, leaving them to do whatever they wished with her. Even with the splitting pain, the beast within her kept her ready to fight. She'd suffer for the hit later, but right now it only enticed her tigress more.

While she blinked to push away the black spots, he took advantage of the situation. He cupped her hand and brought it down to his crotch. "Feel that, bitch. Very soon it's going to make you scream. I'll take you first, last, and everywhere in between. After delivering you to Lorcan, I'm going to make you pay for every time you piss me off. Please, keep it up." He kept a grip on her wrist so she couldn't hurt him. Slowly, he drew her hand along the length, making sure she realized he was well endowed.

"I don't mind seconds, because after the first one has you, most won't care what kind of condition you're in. I can bloody you all I want, and they won't give a shit." He wrapped his other hand around her throat. "You'll be thrilled to know that Omar here is one of the cruelest of the clan when it comes to sex. Only to be outdone by our Alpha. You'll be lucky if you make it out of it with all your body parts intact. Or he might just suffocate you by accident. It's happened before. He loves breath play when it comes to sex."

She couldn't stop the fear rising within her. She had been in that position before, and she didn't want to be there again. Sex with someone other than one's mate was uncomfortable before the mating commenced, even painful for some. After a shifter found their mate the pain from having sex with someone else would be excruciating. She might not have found her mate yet, but she sure as hell didn't want to experience the pain she had before, nor did she want to find out she was destined to be mated with one of the Washington D.C. Tigers. That would be worse than death at her Alpha's hands.

"Not gonna happen," a voice suddenly announced.

Another man came up behind Omar. In a blur, the man who had spoken dashed toward them, tossing her captor across the roof. She grabbed the railing and watched in terror as the scene unfolded. Omar laid in a pile at the other man's feet, blood pouring out of him. She bit back a scream and tried to get her legs to work. She had to get out of there before her saviors became her new problem. Whoever they were, they were dangerous. She had smelled the awful stench of horror from her captor when the man grabbed him. At the very least, they knew of each other. Whatever was there inspired pure fright.

The new arrival pulled out a silver blade. "Now, I believe you threatened the woman with rape, and for that you'll pay."

"You've got it all wrong. She wants it…" Her captor looked to her, his eyes begging for her to back him up.

"Didn't look like it." He twirled the blade as if debating where to stab him.

"She's an unprotected female, which means she's up for grabs. Plus, she came into our territory without permission, so that's a death sentence."

"She's protected now, and as I see it the Washington D.C. Tigers won't have a place much longer. The Queen of the Tigers is taking over and will eliminate you." With that, he flung the knife to land dead center in the man's groin. Howls of pain erupted. "Finish him, Theodore."

It didn't matter that they'd saved her life, she had to get out of there. She had learned more than once that there was no one she could trust. These couldn't have been the men she had been watching because they hadn't had enough time to track her scent from the park bench. *Run.*

Styx turned from the would-be rapist to the tigress they'd been looking for. Without even asking, he knew she was the woman who'd sent the forum the message. Her terror was pungent, more than before, but it wasn't her scent that verified it. It was way she looked at him with both fear and hope.

The wind blew her long black hair around her like a cape, the curls tangling in the wind. Desire to pull it all together and hold it away from her face ate at him. He wanted to see her completely, more of the smoky blue eyes that gleamed out at him. He slid his second knife back into the sheath on his belt and moved forward. Each step was controlled, even as his tiger fought to be released. He held it back, allowing determination into every cell of his body.

She darted away from him and toward the door. Beautiful and terrified. He sidestepped and caught her before she could get past him. He wrapped his arm around her waist, and pulled her against his body. Sparks tingled within him everywhere he touched her. "Whoa, Catnip."

"Please, I don't want any trouble. I'll leave the city." She fought against him, slamming her fists into his chest.

"I'd say you've found enough trouble on your own." He took hold of her wrists to stop the assault. "We're the help you called for. Now, if you'd stop this, I have a few questions."

"The help…" She froze. Questions she hadn't put into words were clear in her eyes.

"Tabitha sent me. I'm a member of the Alaskan Tigers." He mentioned Tabitha with the hopes it would calm her, and it did. She relaxed against his embrace.

"*He's* not a tiger." She nodded to Theodore, who had finished permanently silencing the tiger who had a knife through his manhood. She sniffed the air. "He's a bear!"

"Theodore is part of the Kodiak Bears, our ally," he explained as the other man neared them. "His brothers, Turi and Trey, are the ones who received your transmission. So, though you may think you owe Tabitha and Ty gratitude for sending us here, without the Kodiak Bears we wouldn't have the forum or your transmission."

"I've heard a lot about the Connecticut Tigers, and your Alpha—Frank," Theodore began. "Your Alpha's lies are meant to scare you, to keep everyone devoted to him." He shook his head in disgust. "That bastard's days are numbered."

"What would you know about it?" she snapped.

"Do you think you were the only one?" Styx questioned. "Tabitha has supporters all over the globe and right under the noses of disapproving Alphas."

"Not there." She shook her head, sending strands of her wild hair into Styx's face. "No one helped me. No one there is a supporter."

"Did you tell anyone you were leaving?" When she didn't reply, he continued. "That's why no one helped. No one knew you were in danger. Only Frank and his guards knew where your support was, and how they knew I'm not sure."

"Oh, I know." She pulled from his embrace, stalked over to the railing and stared out over the park and river, her arms crossed over her chest. "My sister told Frank what was going on, because she was trying to avoid punishment for her own crimes."

"Your sister?" Theodore didn't bother to hide his revulsion.

"Not everyone has the devoted family you do, Bear." Styx went to the woman and placed his hand on her shoulder. "Catnip, I'm sorry."

"My name is *not* Catnip. I don't know why you're calling me that." She growled in annoyance.

"Why don't you tell me your name, then?"

"Mira. Just Mira. I've left behind the last of my family when they betrayed me." She rubbed her hand up her arm. "You can't trust anyone."

"You can trust me." He squeezed her shoulder. "I'm going to protect you. We're going to get out of here, but I have one more question." Before she could answer, the roof door opened. Garth and the other man who must have been Red came dashing through. Weapons were drawn and ready for what they expected to be a fight.

She pulled away from him, glancing over the railing, as if for a brief moment she considered jumping. Her fear spiked as she eyed them. There was no doubt she was wondering if they were members of the same clan as the two dead tigers on the ground. Her gaze stayed on Garth, his leather jacket and black jeans failing to help his image.

"It's okay," Styx said quickly. "They're with us. Garth and Red are part of the West Virginia Tigers, and they're here as backup."

"We're here to get your asses out of here. Now that *this* is taken care of and you've found her, let's go." Garth nodded toward the dead bodies. "Cops are out, and within the hour they're going to be setting up roadblocks on every major route out of town. Talk has it that once they've got those shut down, the rest of the routes in and out of town will follow."

"They know we're here," Theodore stated.

"They know there's at least one shifter within their territory without permission, and they believe more from the tigress's clan will follow. Quinn called me when Styx didn't answer his cell phone. His unit has been dispatched to assist. They're calling in all branches of the government with the claim that this was a threat to national security. We've got to get out of town, *now*."

"Give us a minute and we'll be ready." He waited until the others had moved toward the rooftop door before turning his attention back to Mira. "How did you know that code from your transmission?"

"It's hard to explain."

"*Try*, and be quick about it. We don't have time for a long explanation but I need to ensure you're not a security risk before I take you somewhere safe." They might not be heading back to the Alaskan Tigers' compound straight away, but the West Virginia Tigers were an ally and he wouldn't take trouble to their doorstep if he could help it.

"I just *knew*. I don't know how." She dragged her hand through her hair, tugging the long strands away from her face. "Do you know what Mira means?"

"What?"

"My name. Mira. In Spanish, it means *sight*, normally of a firearm but it fits me. I have these dreams that let me know what the future holds. Normally it's just mine or those close to me, but the dream is what showed me the code to send to you. I knew what it meant and that you'd find me. Why?"

"Dreams of the future?" he pressed, instead of answering her question.

"Yes. Not all the time, but I knew you'd find me. Well, not you in particular, but I knew someone from your clan would come for me. I knew it would be on a rooftop just like this, when the moon was just overhead. It's why I came here tonight. I saw you at the park and you found my message, but how did you know I was here? You didn't have enough time to trace my scent, not with all the backtracking I did."

"I'm the best at what I do, that's why the Elders sent me." Now was not the time for him to get into why he knew she'd been on that roof, or the sizzling of electricity that passed through them when they touched. "That code you used is ancient. No one uses it or even knows that language any longer."

"Someone had to or you wouldn't be here."

"That is story for another time. Let's get out of the city, and we can put together a game plan when we get somewhere safe." He placed a hand on the small of her back, and urged her toward the door. The same sizzle from before had returned, tingling through their touch. He knew what it meant, but denied it. He didn't want to entertain that thought, as if just thinking of it might bring it to life more than it already was. The tingling was the first sign, but it was the last thing he needed right now.

Mira sat in the back of the SUV as they raced through the city. The man who had wrapped his arm around her drove while the bear rode shotgun. Now that she was out of immediate danger, she looked at the driver more carefully. His short midnight black hair was neatly cut, almost hiding the slight wave to it, and those green eyes sparkled when he looked at her. Her thoughts returned to how his taut and toned muscles felt against her, and how she'd brushed her hand against his chest.

Despite his exotic good looks, he held an air of danger. There was something that drew her to him, and made her want to run in the opposite direction at the same time. Her mind screamed that he was dangerous. Maybe not in the same way Frank or the Washington D.C. Tigers were, but he was still a threat. She wasn't sure of his name, but at the moment it didn't seem to matter. He hadn't bothered to tell her his name when she had told him hers. She made a mental note to ask him later.

With that, she let her gaze slide to Theodore. The first thing that caught her attention was his shoulder length light brown hair, with mixtures of darker brown highlights. If either of them was less of a threat, based on looks, she'd say it was him. He was younger and seemed to follow the other man's lead. Still, even though she knew the things Frank had said were lies, she couldn't help but feel uncomfortable with the bear in the car. He was the unknown in the equation, the one she feared the most. Especially now that Garth and Red were in the other vehicle. When everyone was together, she wasn't sure if she was more concerned with Garth or Theodore. Garth's leather jacket and black jeans reminded her of the shifters who were killed on the roof.

"Quinn said this route has a road block, so I'm programing a new route into the GPS that he says is clear. It will get us back to the airstrip at the cost of an additional fifteen minutes." Theodore leaned forward and tapped the dashboard screen, readjusting the navigation. He eyed the driver. "You might not like him, my friend, but having him as a United States Marshal can have its benefits."

"Quinn?" Mira questioned tentatively.

"Quinn Evans," the man in the driver's seat replied. "He's a black panther. He's without a clan, but he's a supporter of Tabitha's...in his own way."

With the GPS updated, Theodore turned in his seat to look at her. "Don't mind him, he just doesn't like Quinn's style of doing things."

"Let's just say there's bad blood between us." He never met her gaze in the rearview mirror like he had every other time he'd spoken. Was there something more to this tension between him and the Marshal? She wasn't sure, but it was just one more thing she would have to ask him later.

"Bad blood." Theodore let out a deep laugh. "You can't even be in the same room with him and not clash. We're all on the same side, but you two act like you could kill each other."

"Not all of us are on the same side," he snapped, as the last of the city lights faded behind them. "Don't doubt for one minute that Quinn wouldn't turn one of us in if it meant making his career. Unlike the rest of us, who are fighting for the lives of our entire species, he's all about himself."

They pulled to a stop next to a private plane a short while later, and Theodore opened his door. "I'll get the plane started."

"We'll keep watch while you get us ready," he told the bear shifter as he climbed out.

Since she couldn't hide in the SUV permanently, she followed suit. The cool winter air hit her with full force, and a few snow flurries danced on the air like flakes of glitter scattered through the darkness. The few lights around the small private airport served to make the flakes glisten. She had been entertained briefly by the magic of it, and it wasn't until the man beside her pushed his door shut that she even noticed Theodore had disappeared into the plane, leaving them alone. "You never told me who you are."

"There's a purpose for everything."

Even after she stepped in front of him, he refused to meet her gaze. "You're hiding something."

"Everything I do has a reason. We should go. Garth and Red have arrived at their plane and will be ready to take off shortly." He nodded toward the only other plane on the runway. It was a little farther down, but she could still make out the lights of the truck they had been driving.

"Tell me your name or I'm not going." If he didn't want her to know something as simple as his name, it only made her question what else he was hiding from her.

"Once you know that bit of information, you'll still *claim* you won't be going."

"Claim?" She didn't like how he stressed the word, as if he had already considered other ways of getting her on the plane.

"My word is one thing everyone knows I don't trifle with. If I say I'm going to do something, then consider it done, because the only thing that would stop me is my death. So unless you plan to kill me, you will be on that plane and headed to safety because I vowed to my Elders you would be."

Fear crept up her spine, drying her mouth, and making her palms sweat. She didn't like where this was going, but she was going to follow it to the bitter end regardless of the consequences. "I'll ask you again. What is your name?"

"Styx."

Her legs went limp. If not for his quick reflexes, she'd have been a puddle on the tarmac. "Styx." His name emerged in a rough whisper. *The assassin.*

Chapter Four

Mira was still trying to wrap her head around who he was when he threw her over his shoulder and started toward the plane. Why hadn't she seen it? He was the most respected—and the most feared—assassin of their kind. Frank's words echoed in her mind: *If he comes for you there is no way around your death. If you're lucky he may kill you quickly, but if you anger him he'll drawl it out until you're begging for death. He's a killer through and through. Never doubt that I'll send him after anyone who betrays me.*

"Put me down!" She pounded on his back. "If you're going to kill me, then I demand you look at me while you do it."

"So, we're back to me killing you. That didn't take long." His disgust was clear in his words. "Seems like I never move past that with some people."

"That's why you're here. He warned me, but I didn't listen. I don't know how you intercepted the message, or how you knew I was a supporter of Tabitha, but it doesn't matter now. Just get it over with. I don't like the idea of torture, so could you make it quick?" she snapped, though her voice was beginning to tremble. "I bet Frank is paying you extra to make sure I suffer so he can show the clan what happens to those who betray him."

Inside the plane, he dropped her on the table close to the door so he could keep a grip on her while pulling the steps up and the door shut. "Now, listen to me. I don't know what other lies your Alpha brainwashed you with, but I'm *not* here to kill you. My past might be bloodier than some, but I mean you no harm."

"How am I supposed to believe that?" If she had been a more powerful shifter, she could have smelled the truth on him, but she wasn't. No one from her clan was powerful that way, and if they were they kept it to themselves because Frank would have killed anyone who showed signs of being stronger than him.

"I'll prove it if you promise not to open the door. Theodore is preparing the plane for takeoff. If you try to leave, you'd be walking straight into trouble."

"Or I could already be in trouble."

"If I wanted to take you somewhere else to kill you, I'd have bound you so you couldn't escape or knocked you unconscious. I haven't done anything like that, so give me some credit."

She didn't like the sound of it, but she acquiesced. If he meant her harm, he had plenty of time. After he pulled the steps in completely, she watched her last route of escape close. Her stomach roiled. If he tried to kill her, she would have nowhere to go, especially not once they were in the air. *Please don't let this be a mistake.*

"Will you stop fretting? You're making the air thick with your fear." He tossed his bag on the table beside her and pulled back the flap.

"What are you going to do?" She watched the bag, expecting him to pull out a gun or a torture device.

"My phone screen isn't as big as some of the new ones, so I'm grabbing my laptop. It will give you a much better view, and then you won't suspect I've prerecorded the message or whatever else you could come up with to doubt this." He slid the laptop out of his bag and opened the screen. It flashed to life, awaiting his passcode.

"What would I need to see? What message?" She didn't understand how he was going to prove to her that he wasn't there to kill her, and that only served to make her more nervous. She wanted to hop off the table and pace the interior of the plane.

His long fingers slid over the keyboard with finesse. He wasn't the average assassin who was only familiar with weapons and ways to kill. Computer skills and knowledge of codes wasn't something she would've expected from him. "I'm calling my Elders."

"What? Wouldn't someone be able to trace that? My Alpha might—"

"We've got a secure video conferencing line so we can communicate with our allies as needed." He brought up the screen, and the ringing of a phone echoed out of the laptop's speakers.

"Hello." A man with long black hair stared back at them.

"Mira, this is Raja, the Lieutenant of the Alaskan Tigers. Raja, meet Mira." He gave a quick introduction but didn't give them time to formally say hello. Instead, he continued to the point of the call. "Does Tabitha or Ty have a moment?"

"Little woman giving you trouble?" Raja smirked. "Good for you, girl."

"We could do with less of that, and more of you calling for them," Styx reasoned, as Theodore powered up the engines. "We're on a limited time frame here."

"You interrupted a meeting, so it better be important." Raja handed what appeared to be an e-tablet over to someone else. A moment later, a woman and a man filled the screen.

The woman's strawberry blonde hair was unmistakable, leaving no doubt of her identity. It was as if she'd just stepped out of one of Mira's visions. "You must be the woman who sent the message," Tabitha intoned.

"I'm Mira. It's a pleasure to...um, meet you." That was an understatement. Knowing what Tabitha had done for their kind, and what she intended to do in the future, left her sitting in awe before the Queen of the Tigers. Everything would be vastly different one day. That was a world Mira wanted to live in, so she supported Tabitha in her quest. That was what landed her in this mess in the first place. Things would change for the better one day, and Mira would be a part of it.

"What's this about, Styx?" the man beside Tabitha inquired. "If you've found her, you should be on your way to Jinx."

"Ty," Styx began, his tone bitter. "It would appear Frank has used me to scare his people, threatening to send me after them if they disobey. I assumed my name would instill fear in her, like it does with everyone, so I held off on disclosing my identity until she demanded it. Now that she knows who I am, she believes her Alpha has sent me to torture and kill her."

"What would you like us to do?" Tabitha asked.

"Confirm my status within your clan, and please let her know I'm here on your behalf. I thought this would be the best way to convince her." Styx glanced at Mira, and then back at the screen.

"I could have done that," Raja hollered from somewhere off-screen.

"It wouldn't have been the same." Tabitha adjusted in her seat, and the tablet wobbled some as she leaned back against the sofa. "Mira, I appreciate you being a supporter, though I have to say I apologize it has come at the cost of your clan and home. When we received notification that you were on the run, we sent Styx to find you. He's the best there is."

Mira's eyebrow shot up at Tabitha's choice of words. She had no doubt that he was the best at what he did, but the question was, what did he do *now*? Was he still the assassin history claimed him to be, or was he using his *skills* as a way to protect those who were making things better for their kind?

Tabitha caught her sudden suspicion. "He's the best at what he does," she continued. "And by that, I am not just referring to his methods of protecting people. He's no longer an assassin. Does he still kill people? Yes, but only when there are no other options. He does it to keep us safe, so we can do what needs to be done to ensure our survival."

Ty wrapped his arm around Tabitha's shoulders, slipping back into view. "You might be wondering why we sent him over someone else. Since you decided to go to D.C., we couldn't send a whole team in for you. Limited manpower meant we had to have the best. That's Styx. We knew he'd get you out of the city alive, and hopefully without too much of an issue."

"Only two dead," Styx chimed in. "I'd say that's an achievement considering the circumstances."

"Ignore him." Tabitha shook his head. "He can go without killing anyone, so there must have been danger to you or someone else."

She thought about the roof and what had happened there. As crazy as it sounded, she didn't count those deaths against him. He had saved her life, and possibly saved her from a fate worse than death.

"Styx is an amazing warrior, one we're glad to have on our side. He would not be one of the Elder guards if we doubted for a minute his true nature." Tabitha glanced at Styx before back to Mira. "His history is his to tell, one that I promise you is both bloody and enlightening. Know this: there's more to the man beside you than his skills or his past. Trust him. He'll keep you safe."

"Satisfied?" Styx questioned.

She turned away from the laptop, looked up at him, and smiled. "Thank you." She hopped off the table and let him wrap up the conversation. The plane was full of wood furniture that appeared to be hand-carved, with amazing details. Strolling down the aisle, she ran her hand over the smooth wood. Whoever had spent the time to crave such detail must have a lot of patience.

A few moments later, Styx closed the laptop. "Theodore, we're ready whenever you are."

"Then sit down and buckle up," he called from the cockpit.

Styx nodded to the single row of seats on the plane. "You might want the window so you can see the lights of the city as we take off."

"If I never see D.C. again, I won't be missing anything. You can have it." She sat down in the middle, leaving both the aisle and the window seat available for him to choose.

He took the aisle seat without a word and snapped his seatbelt on.

"How long will the flight to Alaska be?" she asked.

"We're not going to Alaska right away."

"What?"

"Theodore was on his way to the West Virginia Tigers' compound when your message came through. That's why he was the likely choice for backup. As a pilot, he could act as both. Now he has to deliver this furniture to Jinx and Summer. Garth and Red will meet us there as well, but that's their home so they won't continue on with us wherever we go next."

"What do you mean *wherever* we go next? Won't we go to Alaska?"

"I will return there, but we still need to see where the best place is for you. You're still connected to the Connecticut Alpha, so until you've committed yourself to another Alpha, or he has been eliminated, you could be a potential threat to the Elders. It's my responsibility to keep them safe."

"I would not betray—"

"That is not what I meant." Styx stopped her before she could continue. "You have no connections to anyone in the clan. No one to know your true motives. It's only a precaution."

"No connections, huh?" She took his hand in hers, and the heat and tingling returned. "What about this?"

His eyes sparkled with shock before he blinked it away. "That's different."

"I saw the surprise in your eyes. Did you think I didn't feel it? Even with all that was going on, how could I have missed the *mating connection*?"

"If you felt it, how could you think I was sent to kill you? Or worse, that I would torture you?" His eyes closed as Theodore sped the plane down the runway, beginning their takeoff.

"Flying makes you nervous." All her fears and anger slipped away, as she watched him pale before her eyes. She laid her hand over his and squeezed it lightly.

"You didn't answer my question."

"I'm..." She paused and decided it was best to be truthful. "I'm terrified. There's no other way to put it. My mind is jumping from one thing to another. From what I know is true, to what I've seen, to what I've been told. Fear will do crazy things to a person, but when you've witnessed some of the things I have, you know that even a mating doesn't stop evil or wrongdoing."

"I'm not going to hurt you."

"I believe that now." She glanced down. "If you don't ease off that armrest, you're going to do some major damage." When he pried his hand away, she laced their fingers together. "Come on, big bad tiger. Just relax. Flying isn't so awful."

He gave her a grunt and didn't comment. "Once we reach the right altitude, and settle out, I can forget we're thousands of feet in the air. It's only during takeoff and our descent that I can't pretend I'm still on the ground and everything is normal."

"I've heard stories of what you've done," she said, changing the subject. "Maybe some of them have been lies, but not all of them. I saw how the Washington D.C. Tigers looked at you on the roof. They'd have pissed themselves if they had the chance."

"What's your point?" It came out as more of a growl than she had expected, and she almost pulled away.

"I was getting to that. You're the monster under the bed, the proverbial boogieman. Stories about you make everyone look over their shoulders, and listen to their Alphas, otherwise you'll come for them. Yet, you're scared of flying. This fear of yours makes you seem...I don't know, I guess *normal* is the best word. I wouldn't have expected you to be afraid of anything."

"Everyone is afraid of something. Being thousands of feet in the air in a metal box is my fear, because there's nothing I can do if we go down. If I'm going to die, I want a fighting chance." As the plane settled in flight, he opened his eyes and glanced at her. "Trusting my life or the lives of the ones I love to someone else has never turned out well for me."

In his tone she caught a hint that there was more of a story behind his words, but to ask him about it wouldn't ease his tension. "You'd rather be in control." She smirked. "Why am I not surprised at that? But there's something that does surprise me."

"What's that?"

"If you like to be in control, why don't you command your own clan?"

He let out a deep sigh before shaking his head. "You remember your reaction when you heard my name. It's always the same. No matter where I go, the reaction is always the same. There's even some among the Alaskan Tigers who *still* question my loyalty. It's better now, but I know there's some who look at me and see my past or the rumors they've heard. I can never get past it. Who would want me to lead them?"

"You'd be an Alpha who could protect them. I'd give anything to have an Alpha to protect me instead of the one I got saddled with."

"The fear would be there, and some people would question why anyone would follow me." He leaned his head back. "Anyway, I'm happy with my position with Tabitha and Ty."

"Happy doesn't mean it's all you want."

"Now's not the time."

She wasn't sure if he was referring to becoming an Alpha, or the conversation itself. She might have pressed harder, but Theodore interrupted them.

"It should be a quick flight, but if you need to get up, go ahead."

"We're fine. Just want to be there." Styx rolled his shoulders. "All of us are exhausted, so we'll spend the night there and start west after we've slept. I'll speak to Jinx to make arrangements."

"It's too close," Mira said. "What if they've followed? They'll find me."

"No one is going to find you." He squeezed her hand. "You're safe now. I promise."

"They've followed me everywhere so far. Staying with another clan puts them in danger, too." Fear coated her words.

"Jinx is the Alpha of the West Virginia Tigers. His clan is located near Snowshoe, and in order to find it they'd have to know the area. It's desolate, believe me. Even so, there are ground guards, and you'll be safe. He knows the situation. He sent Garth and Red as backup, and they're prepared. Relax. Let me do the worrying. I promised I'd keep you safe, and I'll stick to my word."

The terror rose within her, and she tried to stuff it aside. Styx's fear of flying had already tinted the air with a rancid scent. She didn't need to add to it. She asked for help, and now she had it, so she'd have to trust them—even if it went against everything inside of her.

Trusting people had brought her to this situation in the first place. What horrors would befall her next because she placed her trust in someone? Would Styx end up dead because he helped her? The very thought of someone losing their life because of her made her ill.

What have I done?

Chapter Five

The airplane came to a stop, and relief coursed through Styx's veins. There'd be another plane trip in a few hours, but to be back on the ground again was all he could focus on. Tomorrow he'd worry about the longer trip back across the country. Mira had made him consider the humor in his fear, but if there was one thing he'd learned about things that terrified someone, it was they didn't have to make sense. When it was someone's time to die, they did, and nothing could be done to stop death. Even shifters weren't immune to death.

He unclicked his seatbelt, stood, and held his hand out to Mira. "Come on. It's going to be okay."

"I don't like the idea of endangering others."

"Even so, you wanted our help, so let me do my job."

"Is that *all* I am to you? A job?"

He could hear the pain in her voice, but wasn't sure how to answer her question. If he said yes, he'd be denying the mating connection that was blooming between them. On the other hand, if he said no he would be accepting that she was to be his mate. Was he ready for that? He wasn't sure. It was a question that would require thought and exploration.

"The clan Elders are waiting," Theodore hollered back to them as the engines shut down.

"We can't keep them waiting."

She rose from the chair and zippered her jacket. "I guess that's enough of an answer."

He slipped his bag over his shoulder and reached for her, but she pulled back from him. "It's not what you think."

"What am I thinking? Can you read minds or something?" she remarked snidely.

He shook his head. That was one ability he'd never want. "Catnip, you're very easy to read."

"I know. It's gotten me in trouble with my Alpha in the past." She slipped her hands into the pockets of her coat, and met his gaze. "Why do you call me *Catnip*?" she asked tentatively.

"Beautiful Mira, your scent is to my tiger as catnip is to kittens." He wrapped his hand around her wrist and pulled her against him. "That, Catnip, should answer your question. I can't get enough of you."

"One minute, you act one way…and the next you act differently. It's confusing."

"Let's meet with the Elders of the West Virginia Tigers, and then we can talk more about this. We don't know each other at all, so things are bound to be uncertain. We have to overcome a few things, for starters." He stepped away from her, and pushed down the planes steps. "First of all, you'll have to trust me. The compound here is safe, Jinx has ground guards on the perimeter, and I'm not going to let anything happen to you."

"Trusting someone has been disastrous for me in the past."

He leaned close to whisper in her ear. "I know you trusted someone with your secret and they betrayed you, leaving you no choice but to run for your life. But that brought you to me, and I'd rather fall on my blade than deceive someone on our side. I will not betray you."

"My sister…she's young and naive. She thought it would save her."

He glanced at her one last time, and saw the tears shinning in her eyes. She was on the verge of a breakdown. Was it just because of what her sister done and what that decision had cost her? "It didn't, though, did it?"

"Now's not the time." She nodded toward where he knew Jinx and the others were waiting. "Let's go, and I'll explain later."

He wanted to force the subject, but common sense won out. To leave Jinx and the others waiting outside as he questioned Mira further would not only be rude, but uncalled for. There'd be time for it once they were inside, after he explained the situation to Jinx so he could alert his guards. He tugged his bag up his shoulder, and descended the stairs.

"It's good to see you again, Jinx." Styx held out his hand to the man waiting below. "Thank you for opening your compound to us. This is Mira, and Theodore will be along in a moment. Mira, this is Jinx, his mate, Summer, and their daughter Claire." He nodded to the woman who held a toddler in her arms.

She lowered her head as if to respectively nod, but it was the curtsy that followed that had Styx taken aback. It had been centuries since anyone curtsied for ruling Alphas. That had been done away with since Alphas had their members vow their loyalties, creating the bond between them. That's when they had done away with some of the barbaric rituals of their past.

"There's no need for that." Jinx smirked, and adjusted his cowboy hat. "We'd don't do that anymore." He appeared curious, and just as surprised as Styx.

Styx wasn't surprised that Jinx's comments mirrored his very thoughts. If Styx had followed another Alpha, it surely would have been Jinx. They were similar in many ways, but the biggest was that they both fought feverishly for what they believed in.

"I apologize…" Seeming uncertain, she bit the corner of her lip. "My Alpha requires it any time you're in his presence."

The men shared a look as Lukas joined them, his red hair sparkling as fresh snow fell on the moist locks. "Are we going to stand out here in the cold all night? Come inside. Garth and Red will be here in a few minutes, and will meet us inside."

"My Lieutenant has a point. We'll warm up, and you can bring me up to speed on the situation." Jinx slipped his arm around Summer's waist and turned.

"Can I have a moment, Styx?" Mira placed her hand on his arm.

"We'll meet you inside in a moment with Theodore," Styx told them as the others headed toward the building in the distance. "What's wrong?"

"How come you didn't tell me they had a child? We're not only risking Jinx's clan, but his mate and that little girl. What is she, a year old? How can I risk her, just so that I'm safe?"

"Claire is two and has been through hell and back. They rescued that child from the Texas Tigers' former Alpha, where he had her hidden away in the tunnels under the Manetka Resort. They've taken her in as they own."

"What about her parents?" She glanced toward the receding backs of Jinx and the others.

"Her father, Cliff, abandoned his clan and children. Claire's older sister is Ashley, she's mated and recently had her first child. They are unable to care for Claire in her current condition." He held out his hand before she could ask. "She's rarely spoken since she saw her mother murdered before her eyes. She's attached to Summer, and has made some progress since she came here with them."

For a brief moment, he was taken back to that mission to eliminate Avery, the former Texas Tigers' Alpha. Jinx had risked himself to go undercover in the resort to try to determine which underground passages might lead them to Avery. That mission had brought Jinx his mate, but at the cost of Summer's sister. So many had died at Avery's hands, but no longer. Jinx had killed him, and Tex had taken over the clan.

"I heard about what happened in Texas. You killed the Alpha." The accusation was clear in her voice.

"You heard what Frank wanted you to know. Otherwise, you'd realize it was Jinx who actually killed Avery." He paused to let that sink in before explaining what led to his death. It wasn't just that they stormed the place and killed him while he was lying in bed. Would they have done that? Hell yes, because of what he was doing to his clan, but that wasn't the way it went down. "When we arrived at Manetka Resort and entered the underground tunnels, Avery had a woman stretched out on a table with members of his clan watching her torture. That woman was Autumn, Summer's sister. Jinx didn't know that Summer was his mate yet, but none of us would have let Avery live after what he had done to her. She wasn't the first victim, but we made sure she was the last."

"Frank and Avery were close," Mira said. "I won't say friends because I'm not sure Frank lets anyone close enough to be considered a friend. He believes you're coming for him."

"Now we are." Styx looked up as Theodore exited the plane.

"Just like Avery, Frank made his choices and we'll have to make ours," Theodore said, coming down the steps. "There are other supporters within your clan who will need to be freed. It's doubtful he'll step aside and let someone else take over. That will be his undoing."

"Mira, we can't leave Alphas who are against Tabitha and the prophesied future in a position of power. Anyone who does not support a future with Tabitha as the Queen of the Tigers is an enemy." He touched her arm, slowly caressing his way up to her shoulder. "We're doing this for the betterment of our kind. Alphas like Avery and Frank should have been eliminated by their clan long before but they gained control. Now, the clans are too scared to fight back."

"They've seen too much bloodshed and torture. Even death…and we're hard to kill."

Even without the mating connection being complete, he could feel the horror surface within her. What terrors had she witnessed over the years since Frank had become Alpha? "When you're one of us, you already know our weaknesses. When there's an Alpha with a clan too scared to stop him, there's nothing holding him back from the evil within him."

"Now it's our job to stop them," Theodore added, as he closed the plane up.

"There's more to it than that, but the bear's right. Tabitha will be protected, and we'll make sure the future happens no matter the cost, because we realize what it will do to our kind. Since your Alpha seems to share gossip, did he tell you about the Minnesota Tigers?"

"You mean that Milo, one of the bears, and a human who went and killed the Alpha?" Her tone was flat, as if what she said didn't matter, even though her eyes said otherwise. "After we were told about that, it was the first time my sister questioned how I could support Tabitha and what was happening. Frank made her and the others believe you were killing Alphas to put your own men in control."

"Then he left something out," Styx said. "Christian was born and raised among the Minnesota Tigers. Until Milo, Thaddeus, and Courtney came along, none of us had met him, and they had already planned to take Calvin from his role of Alpha. So, we haven't been setting our own people up as Alphas."

"What about Ohio? One of the Alaskan Tigers took over the role of Alpha there when Randolph killed the former leader."

Styx nodded. "True, but that was because no one within the clan was in the right mind frame to do it. Like the Texas Tigers, they had suffered under the hands of their Alpha too long. Korbin went there to take over and pull the pieces back together. Jinx went with him to help. He's done wonders for that clan, even though he was not a member to start with. Even now, they've begun construction on the old warehouse just south of the Ohio compound to build a resort similar to Manetka. It will be a safe place for shifters as well as provide more space for his clan."

"Those on the run, like you, would have a safe place to go to receive help," Theodore added. "All of us working together will make for a safer world."

"It would have been nice to know there was somewhere safe to go once I left my clan. I didn't know where to go, so I went to the only place I could think of. I went to Washington D.C. when I was very little. I remembered wandering away from Mom while we were sightseeing, and she freaked out. Even with her heightened scenes of smell, she couldn't find me in the mix of all the tourists. I was hoping it would have been the same with whoever Frank sent after me, and that help would arrive first." A shiver passed through her, making her tremble.

"We did, Catnip, and you're safe." He pulled her against his body. "We're going to deal with Frank, but first I want to get you somewhere safe."

"Getting me to safety might cost others their lives. There's been enough bloodshed because of me."

"Because of you?" Theodore stepped closer to them. "Is there something you're not telling us?"

"Things were a mess when I took off. It's the only reason I was able to escape." The snow picked up again, sending flurries dancing around them.

"Let's go inside and you can explain what happened." Styx mentally berated himself for not questioning her further on their flight, but with her safely next to him all he could think about was the fact they were in the air. Normally, when he flew he had his mind on something, or if they were on their way back from a mission everyone was so exhausted it didn't matter if they were in the air or on the ground all their brains could focus on was sleep.

Maybe the mating desire was building within him enough that he wasn't as focused as he should have been. That bothered him more than anything, because he had to be at his best if he was going to protect her and do his job for the Alaskan Tigers. Mating wouldn't change his duties. He owed everything to Ty, Tabitha, and Shadow for giving him a second chance. One that allowed him to put his skills to use for a good cause, instead of being an assassin. That was something that meant more to him than he'd have admitted—until Mira strolled into his life.

With Styx's arm around Mira's waist, she had no choice but to move with him as he began the trek after Jinx and the others. She could see the footprints in the snow, leading the way to the house that sat slightly elevated above the rest. She glanced around the property, but it was the home that drew her attention more than anything.

"That's the Elders' house. Jinx's family has taken over the third floor, with his Lieutenant, Lukas, living on the second. Two of the Elder guards, Jackson and Carson, are on the first floor," Styx explained, seeming to realize her fascination with the house.

From outside, the building he indicated looked huge. It was a three-story log home, towering over all the others. A beautiful winding pathway led to the houses below, with shrubs that probably flowered in the summer. Snow covered the grounds as far as the eye could see, and seemed to be almost completely undisturbed. In the mountains, they had gotten more snow than she'd seen in D.C., and with the late hour it appeared flawless.

She climbed the few steps, and someone she didn't recognize opened the door for them. His black jeans and t-shirt made the silver butt of the gun in his holster stand out.

"Come in. Jinx and the others are gathered in the living room." He nodded to the right before he held out his hand. "Styx, it's good to see you."

"You too, Carson." He shook the offered hand, before leading her to the living room.

As they entered, all gazes focused on them, making an uneasiness rise within her. Instead of focusing on them, she glanced around the space. The main floor of the Elders' house was simple and beautiful at once. Judging by the pictures on the wall, and the various knickknacks, it was clear many generations had lived here.

"Mira." Styx rubbed her back, soothing her. "You've already met Jinx, but let me introduce you to the others. Lukas, the Lieutenant of the West Virginia Tigers and Jinx's younger brother."

The man with short red hair nodded to her and she recognized him as the one who suggested they head inside. "Summer will be joining us in a few minutes. She's putting Claire back to bed. She only brought her to meet the plane because she woke up with a nightmare a few minutes before you landed."

"It might be best if she stays with the child." Styx eyed Jinx. "If we brought danger to your clan, I'd prefer they were safe."

"Meshell is upstairs with Claire. Jackson and Carson are here as well to protect Summer and Claire," Jinx explained. "No one is going to get onto my land, let alone upstairs, without us knowing about it."

"I hate that I brought you into this mess I've created," Mira said. "Danger, blood, and death follow me and I brought it to your home."

"Catnip, we talked about this." Styx tried to soothe her, but the rage was boiling within her.

"Mira." Another man's voice forced her to look up. She couldn't remember being introduced to him, but she had seen him on the runaway.

"Jackson is the Captain of Summer's Guards," Styx provided as he led her toward the sofa.

"Our compound is over nine hundred and fifty acres, and we've got every inch of it covered. There are guard houses around the perimeter, and they are always manned. We knew you were arriving and we've taken precautions, including alerting everyone on duty to be on the lookout for anything unusual. Every part of the border is covered with motion sensors, heat sensors, and cameras. No one can get on or off this property without us being alerted."

"He should know, he helped design the security." Jinx leaned forward. "Mira, we're far enough away from any roads or houses that we're never bothered. You can't just stumble upon this place. You have to know what you're looking for to end up here. The guards are well trained to protect the border and the clan. We built this building in the center of the land, at the safest point, for a reason. From here, we can see almost the whole compound. If anyone tries to come here, we'll know about it long before they reach us. We can be prepared."

"Still, I risked your mate and child, and that's unacceptable."

"Do you think you're the first hint of danger that's come to our doorstep?" Jinx smirked. "I've allied my clan with the Alaskan Tigers. Their enemies are ours. That means the Alpha of the Connecticut Tigers is my problem. He knows where my clan stands and if he chooses to send his men here, he also knows what kind of fate they will meet."

"Jinx, I know you will say it's unnecessary, but thank you for this. You've opened your home to us and provided us with safety for the night, but tomorrow we will leave." Styx glanced at Theodore who stood off to the side of the sofa where they sat. "We'll sleep, then unload the furniture and leave."

"We've prepared a cabin for you and you're more than welcome to stay as long as you need." Jinx glanced to Theodore. "Thank you for bringing the furniture. Summer has been looking forward to it."

"We'll look it over in the morning and make sure it's everything she wanted." Theodore tried to stifle a yawn but failed.

Styx cleared his throat and brought the attention back to them. "Before everyone gets some sleep, Mira started to tell us more about what was happening in Connecticut before she left. It might give us some insight on what Frank is preparing. So, Mira, if you would continue?"

"Umm…" No longer could you put off the whole story, but nervousness had her stuttering.

"It's okay, just take your time." Styx took her hand into his and gave it a light squeeze. The electricity passing through them grew stronger with each touch, and would continue to until they finalized their mating.

"My sister got caught doing something she wasn't supposed to, and instead of just handling things she thought if she told our Alpha something worse, he'd forget about what she did and go after the other person. But she didn't have dirt on anyone other than me. Some say that blood is thicker than water, but not with my family. She betrayed my trust to save herself from punishment, even when she knew my cost would be higher and that he'd demand my death."

"What did she do?" Jackson asked, and when she glared at him he added, "You implied he wouldn't kill her for it, and since we're trying to get into his mindset it might be helpful to know the full story."

"She wouldn't have been killed for sneaking out of the compound that night because his son was with her. If he killed her, one of the clan could demand that he kill the other. He'd never jeopardize his own son." She paused for a moment and took a deep breath, the memories making her body shake as if she was cold. "He had planned to dish out punishment to her for leading his precious son astray, so the clan was gathered together to watch as she met her fate."

"And that fate would have been…?" Styx pushed when she went silent again.

"It was set up for a beating. He'd have flogged her until there wasn't any skin left on her back or her ass. I realize that's painful because I've had it done to me, but to get out of it by betraying me and therefore calling for my death was unexpected. She knew what the consequences of her actions would be if she got caught, but still she left the compound without permission." Her chest shook as she tried to keep the tears from falling. "I guess the same could be said about me, because I knew what would happen if he ever found out I supported Tabitha."

"Okay, to get out of her punishment, she told Frank about you. What happened?" Jinx asked.

"I was near the back of the crowd, with David, my brother, beside me, and he shoved me toward the door with the order to run. That's when all hell broke out. Frank declared that not only would I be killed for my betrayal, but my whole family would be. I could hear my sister scream, begging for her life, but instead of going back to offer myself up in exchange for my family's lives, I ran." No longer able to hold back the tears, she sobbed. Her body shook, her chest tightening, and her breath was stolen from her lungs with the power of guilt. "How could I have let my family die for my beliefs? What kind of person does that?"

"You don't know they're dead," Summer stated, and until then Mira hadn't even realized she had joined them.

"I do." She took a deep breath, forcing the air into her lungs and letting it out again. "I see things. I knew it was coming, but I refused to believe my sister would betray me in such a way."

Styx pulled her into his lap. "Catnip, this isn't your fault. We'll see that Frank pays for what he did, but don't go writing off your whole family until we know for certain."

"The gunfire and the screams…" She shook her head, sending her hair flying into her face, but she didn't bat it away. "I've no doubt that more than just my family was killed because of me. I confided in her because we're sisters and she was my best friend."

"I know it's no consolation, but I'm sorry," Summer said. "If you ever need to talk, I'm available. My sister, Autumn, was killed by the former Texas Tigers' Alpha before help arrived." She moved across the room and sat down beside Jinx. "That was when Jinx, Styx, and the others came to the clan's rescue, and to my rescue. Jinx killed Avery and set the Texas Tigers free. To set me free."

"Ty and Tabitha put one of their clan members in the position of Alpha over the clan as well." Her voice was still full of tears.

"Tex is the Alpha of my former clan, and he was from the clan originally."

"Summer's right." Styx nodded. "Tex was sent to watch Adam's helicopter when he came to Texas to recuse Robin. He was shot and nearly killed, leaving Adam no choice but to toss him into the 'copter and fly him back to the Alaskan Tigers compound to be healed. That's how we found out what was happening there."

"So, you didn't place your own man as Alpha?"

"No." Styx ran his hand down her arm. "Tex was elected by the clan and he chose his Lieutenant, Ben. Ben is Summer's brother."

"Lies. Why am I surprised all he's told my clan were lies?" She let her head rest against his chest and tried to come to the terms with everything she had learned. Her clan had submitted to Frank because he brainwashed them. People died because of those same words. If there was anyone left from her clan, she had to do something to save them.

Chapter Six

It had taken over an hour for Mira to drift off to sleep, but Styx had done his best to soothe her, rubbing her back and giving her comfort. He could feel her exhaustion, but she had been too upset to sleep. Tears had fallen until she had no more left to cry, and there had been nothing he could do for her. He didn't have the answers as to what happened to her family, but he was determined to find out.

He pushed a strand of her black hair from the side of her face and glanced down at her. Soundly asleep, her chest rose and fell in perfect rhythm. She was his, and all he could think was that he didn't deserve someone like her. His past had been shady at best and downright diabolical at the worst of times. He had killed more than he cared to remember or even admit to himself. All of them were ordered executions, but had the reason for their deaths been legitimate?

Now that he had time to think back to the orders, he doubted it. His former Alpha had been suspicious of everyone, and thought there were things going on behind his back. He was young, and the Alpha had taken him under his wing, giving him a place to live when he would have otherwise been out in the cold without a clan. In return, Styx had done what he was ordered, never bothering to question things until much later. That was when their relationship changed, but in the end it hadn't been Styx who'd plunged the knife into his heart, but another man.

Mira's earlier words played in his thoughts. *You're the monster under the bed, the proverbial boogieman. Stories about you make everyone look over their shoulders, and listen to their Alphas, otherwise you'll come for them.* She hadn't realized how deeply those words cut or how given the chance he'd rather be anyone else. He was an assassin because there had been no other option. He was a pre-teen when the training began, and each day it started before dawn and lasted long past the state of exhaustion. Each moment broke him a little more, but that had been the goal. They'd break him and then build him back into the man, or rather killing machine, that they wanted.

Though he had been ready to leave that life behind, no matter the cost, when his Alpha had been killed, it was a shock that left him lost for a time. He had wandered alone, unsure of what to do. It wasn't until Ty had found him that he seemed to find a new cause to focus on. Instead of using his skills to eliminate a target, he was able to use them to better his kind. He joined Ty's clan, and hadn't regretted it. His past came up often, especially since he had become an Elder guard. Most questioned how he could be trusted, but Ty, Raja, and their mates didn't question him. They knew what he was capable of, and were glad to have him on their side.

He eased out of bed and grabbed his cell phone. He'd contact Ty and see what information he could gather on the state of the Connecticut Tigers. If he had to go to Connecticut himself, he'd find out what the fate of the clan was. He wouldn't leave her with unanswered questions. Until she knew, she couldn't make peace with the choices she'd made and where they brought her.

His cell phone vibrated in his hand. With one last glance at his sleeping mate, he checked the phone. A text from Ty flashed on the screen. *Grab Theodore. Online in ten minutes, we need to talk.*

"Great, what's going on now?" he muttered, before grabbing the bag he'd left on the dresser. He headed to the living room, which was the only other room in the cabin. It was also where Theodore had decided to sleep. Though

Jinx had offered another cabin for Theodore, he had not taken it, opting to stretch out on the sofa. Even though he was the youngest of the Brown brothers, he had their determination and protectiveness coursing through him.

In the living room, Styx pulled the laptop from the bag and sat it on the counter before turning the pot of coffee on. He'd need caffeine to keep him going much longer, and to stop him from returning to the bedroom to snuggle with Mira.

"What's up?" Theodore rolled onto his back to look toward the small kitchenette.

"Ty sent a message. He needs us online now."

"Pour me a cup of that as well." He stretched his arms over his head and let out a yawn. "No sleep for the almighty fighting force."

"That's one way to put it, I guess." He paused the coffee maker to pour two cups. "I know that one day everything we do will be worth it, and I never doubt it."

"But?" Theodore pushed.

"Do you ever wonder how many will survive to see the glorious future?"

"You're thinking about her family. Your mate's grief is tingling within you. Even without the full connection, it's tainting your outlook." Theodore rose from the sofa and came to the bar area where the laptop was booting up. "She'll get through this with your help, and then you'll be back to your old self."

"What if it's brought a new light to my outlook? I never had a family to grieve over and the ones I care about most are the ones I'm protecting. If something happens to them, it's because I didn't do my job. It would be my fault."

"We've always known death would be a part of this. We also knew it was possible we'd be killed before we could succeed. However, we've always been willing to risk that for the future of our kind. Think of the future generations and all we're giving them. Death will come to us all at some point, and yes, it's awful what happened in Connecticut, but it's also the reason we're doing this. We can't leave Alphas like that in command. During his rule, how many people do you think he killed?"

"More than half the clan." Mira stood in the doorway with a blanket wrapped around her shoulders.

"You should be resting." Styx handed Theodore a cup of coffee. "We didn't mean to wake you."

"I felt you get out of bed, and when you didn't come back I wanted to see what was happening."

"We're about to have a video conference with Ty. He knows you're safe, but there are a few things we must deal with." Not that he even knew what they were. "I'll be back in shortly if you want to try to rest."

"I guess." She pulled the blanket tighter around her shoulders.

"Mira?" Theodore called to her before she went back into the bedroom. "He's not trying to get rid of you. If you want to stay, I don't see any reason you can't. If Ty needs to discuss anything privately, you'd have heard from the bedroom anyway."

"I don't want to intrude. It's just kind of weird…"

"What is, Catnip?" Styx pressed when she stopped mid-sentence.

"Being alone. I don't think in my whole life I've ever been alone. Frank allowed every family an apartment of sorts, but it was just one room and a bathroom. There was no privacy, and nowhere to go to get away from everyone. I feel so alone now."

He set his coffee mug aside and crossed the space between them in two quick strides. He wrapped his arms around her and pulled her against his body. "You're not, Catnip. I'm here. You're part of something bigger now."

"But it's gone…my connection to the clan. There's nothing there."

If the connection was gone, it could mean one of two things. Either Frank had shunned her and broken the connection between her and the clan, or he was dead. Even if another shifter had taken over the clan, she wouldn't be connected until she vowed her commitment to the new Alpha. He wasn't sure which one she was hoping for, but he hoped it meant Frank was dead. They wouldn't have to deal with eliminating another shifter. It would also be better for the clan if they finally took things into their own hands.

"I realize it's a shock, but that could be a good thing." Theodore spoke before Styx's glare could silence him.

"What do you mean?" she snapped. "I'm alone because my whole clan is dead...my family."

"Even though he should have kept his mouth shut. That's not what he meant. What he's trying to say is that it's possible Frank is dead. It could mean your clan is free."

"They're free in death," she snapped before looking up at him. "I *know* they're dead."

"You've seen it in your visions?"

"No. I just know it." Her voice broke and she leaned against him. "I close my eyes and I see my whole clan dead, but they're not visions...more like nightmares. He'd have killed anyone he thought was against him, anyone he thought knew my secret but didn't tell him, and most importantly he'd have killed my family because he'd blame them. How am I supposed to think anything else?"

He tried to give her comfort, but he had no idea what she was going through. The family aspect had never been something he'd had to deal with. The closest thing he could compare it to was how he'd feel if something happened to Ty, Tabitha, or one of the other Elders of the Alaskan Tigers. They were his family in a way, but it was more than that because it was his job to protect them. She didn't have that sense of safety when it came to her family, especially not after her sister betrayed her. They might be human most of the time, but their beast within could never forgive a betrayal like that. Even if her human side wanted to forgive and move on, her beast would never give her the satisfaction. Once they betrayed you, they were the enemy. They wouldn't get a second chance to turn against the beast.

"Styx?" Ty's voice came through the laptop speakers.

"We're here, sir." He pressed his lips to her forehead in a light kiss. "It's going to be okay, Catnip. I'll find out what happened to your family and your clan. Trust me."

"Is everything okay there?"

"An emotional roller coaster, that's all," Theodore explained. "Styx's handling it."

"Styx...Mira..."

A woman's voice called out, and Styx had to glance at the screen to be sure it was Bethany. The voice was softer than normal, but it was the tear stained cheeks that made his beast rise within him. "Is everything okay?" He stepped forward, and since his arm was still around Mira, she moved with him.

"Please let me handle this." Raja put his arm around his mate's shoulder.

"What's happened?" Mentally, he calculated how long it would take them to fly back to Alaska.

"Nothing as bad as you're thinking," Raja reassured him.

"I'm sorry, but hearing about this..." Bethany glanced at her mate as if she was worried she'd said something she shouldn't have. "It just brought back memories of my own family."

"Mira, come sit." Theodore pulled out a bar stood for her.

"Come on." Styx waited for her to have a seat before turning his attention to his Alpha. "We're all tired, and it's the middle of the night, so I'll cut straight to the point. What's the reason for this urgent conference call?"

"We've received a call from the Connecticut Tigers."

Ty stopped as Mira's shoulders sank and tears rolled down her cheeks. Styx wasn't used to dealing with women when they were emotional. The only women he'd been around long enough to see them like that were Tabitha and Bethany, and since they were both mated it wasn't his job to comfort. Now, he was neck deep and without a manual to see his way through these turbulent seas.

"Both of you look like you've just received the worst news," Theodore said to Styx and Mira, as he leaned against the counter, his hip brushing against the lip of the countertop so that he could see both them and the computer screen. "Don't you realize what that means?" He didn't wait for them to answer before adding, "There's at least one person from the clan alive, probably more."

"What does it matter if my family is dead?"

Styx rubbed her shoulders, giving her what support he could as he glanced at the screen. "For Mira's sake, let's not draw this out any longer. Who contacted you and what do you know?"

"David." Ty's gaze was only on Mira. "He claims to be your brother."

"He..." Her voice broke with tears. "He's alive?"

"He is." Ty nodded. "He's very eager to find you. I'm afraid there was much death on both sides of the fight, but there's a new Alpha of the clan now."

"The rest of my family? Frank?"

"I can only tell you that Frank has been eliminated. David has asked that he be the one to fill you in on everything else. He's asked that you come home."

"But...I've..." She tipped her head to look up at Styx.

He reached up and laid a hand on the side of her face. His thumb slid over her cheek, brushing away the tears that had fallen, as he stared into the smoky blue eyes that were pleading for his help. "It's okay."

"Am I missing something?" Ty questioned.

Styx forced his gaze back to the computer screen to face his Alpha. If there was one thing Ty didn't like, it was being kept in the dark. "She's to be my mate."

"Congratulations." Tabitha's voice held a hint of excitement.

"To be?" It was Ty who caught the wording.

"I only found her hours ago, and we've been busy."

"You had the plane ride. It would have been the perfect way to distract yourself from the flight," Ty reminded him. "I remember when I first discovered Tabby and realized she was my mate. Even with the danger we were in, and Pierce on our trail, I wanted nothing more than to claim her."

Styx still wasn't sure how he felt about all of it. His human side wanted to push her away, to protect her from his past and from the fear and hatred many had toward him. His enemies were numerous and once they were mated they'd seek her out just as they sought him. She'd be in danger because of who and what he was. Even with all that, the beast within wanted to pull her close and devour her. Torn between the two sides, he wasn't sure which would win.

"I believe the timing hasn't been right," Theodore offered when neither of them said anything.

"He's right." Mira nodded. "I've been wrapped up in my grief and guilt over what happened. Styx has been understanding and comforting. Even though both of our beasts are raging within, and the desire is getting stronger, he hasn't pushed."

"We'll complete our mating when the time is right for both of us, not when the beasts demand it."

"Let me put it this way. She's still technically a member of the Connecticut

Tigers, and if the mating isn't complete by the time you arrive there, it could make things more challenging."

"If you wish to protect her, then you'll complete the mating before you leave West Virginia," Raja added. "Otherwise, the new Alpha could seek retribution for her role in what happened."

"Who's the new Alpha?" She wasn't sure she really cared, because no matter what happened, there was no way she'd ever return to Connecticut.

"David," Ty provided.

"He's my brother, he wouldn't…"

"His role has changed, and even though he would protect you, it doesn't mean that the clan wouldn't demand satisfaction for what happened." Styx squeezed her shoulder. "I know what you're about to say, but their freedom from Frank might not mean the same to them. He might have been vindictive, but he must have also had supporters within the clan, or else he wouldn't have been able to take this much control."

She sat there for a moment, obviously digesting what he had said before she gave a small nod. "Frank never trusted anyone enough to have a Lieutenant, but if he had, David would have been it. He was Frank's right hand man when it came to almost anything."

"Has he committed to our cause?" Styx asked trying to determine just how much a threat David was.

"Not at this time," Ty said. "He has asked for additional time to make the decision so that he could determine how much of a clan he has left. My understanding is that there was death on both sides, and there are some who are only clinging to life. If their will is strong enough, they'll come back from whatever happened. But if they're true supporters of Frank's, they might give up and die with their Alpha."

"He had much to deal with, and while I think he might commit to me as the Queen of the Tigers, he had other things that required his attention at the moment."

"Or he could be buying time to organize his clan for an attack," Raja offered.

"So, if we go to Connecticut, there could be an attack waiting for us." Theodore summarized the last several moments of the conversation into one statement, and unfortunately he was right.

"There could be." Ty nodded. "David could have planned this so that you'd bring Mira home, and then kill you. Styx, I believe you have some reputation with the clan, do you have any idea why? Have you had a run-in with them before?"

"It's because of what Frank said about him," Mira said. "Styx's name was used as a threat. If we didn't fall into line and obey every command that was given, he claimed Styx would kill us. It wasn't until after I met him that I realized all of it was a lie."

"All of it?" He looked down at her questioningly.

"Sometimes a member would go missing from the clan, and Frank would say, *see what happens when you don't listen to me. Styx comes for you.* But in reality, he was the one behind the disappearances. Things I heard over the years, and comments David made…I never put them together until it was too late. Frank was taking those who stood against him to one of the soundproofed rooms he used for punishments. He would torture them until he finally killed them. Sometimes we'd wake to find them strung up in one of the common areas for all to see, and he'd leave them there until they began to rot."

"Then the visit with Styx at your side is going to be much more dangerous," Ty said. "We don't know the full situation there, so if you choose to go, we won't know until you arrive what issues might come up. I'm sure Jinx would loan you additional guards for the journey, or I can send backup and they should be there midday."

"I know the situation has changed, since David is now the Alpha of the clan, but I still don't believe my brother would request my presence only to kill me."

"There are more ways to hurt you than to kill you. If he knows you're with me, he'll see whatever he has planned as a way to protect you from the evil within me." He pulled his hands away from her but didn't step back. "Even if David isn't a threat, my enemies are numerous and there's no doubt I have some among his clan. If they know you're to be my mate, things could get dicey."

"Not *could*." Raja shared a glance with Ty, who nodded. "If you're going, you need to be mated. Styx, you're too important to the clan to risk things. Finalize the mating and go to Connecticut, or fly home. Those are your options. We won't risk you going into an unknown clan's compound, especially with only Theodore as backup."

"Is that a direct order?" Styx raised an eyebrow at them. He understood his position in the clan, and their future, but he hadn't expected them to give him a choice like that. They should have known he'd take every precaution so he would make it safely back to the clan and continue his duty. He'd see that Theodore made it home safely as well. Even if the young bear didn't see it that way, he was Styx's responsibility.

"If it needs to be, then yes." Ty dragged his hand through his shoulder length black hair.

Mira turned on the stool to look up at him. "You said you're an Elder guard...so it's only reasonable. They need you, and you have a job to do."

"Shall we send additional guards to accompany you?" Raja leaned back against the chair and put his arm around Bethany. "If so, we'll need to determine who and get them ready."

"Everyone needs some sleep, so why not reconvene in the morning?" Theodore suggested. "Don't worry about the guards at the moment. I'm sure we can obtain some from Jinx if they decide to do what is necessary and make the journey."

"Very well. I want to know what the plan is by ten tomorrow morning. Jinx is kindly putting you up for the night, but if there's to be additional issues with the Connecticut Tigers, I'd prefer to have you off the east coast. Right now you're just a plane trip away."

Raja cleared his throat when Ty leaned forward as if to end the transmission. "There's just one more thing I'd like to add. Styx, you're important to me when it comes to keeping my mate safe, and you're the perfect partner with Shadow."

"But?"

"But if you think you can deny the mating bond, you're going to end up losing more than just the woman beside you. You won't be able to focus on your duties, and will no longer be able to protect Bethany, or anyone for that matter. You won't be the same unstoppable force that has always been there when we needed you, and you won't be able to have Shadow's back when she needs you, either. You'll be giving up everything you've worked for. So, before you look at her with questions about this mating, I suggest you consider how much you're willing to give up simply because you don't believe you're worthy of the gift that is before you."

The computer screen returned back to the desktop, but even then Styx couldn't pull his gaze away from it. Anger heated his body and his tiger paced inside him. He was livid, which was stupid because Raja's words were the truth. It just wasn't what Styx wanted to hear. The pending mating was throwing him off-balance, but as long as they denied the waiting bond, it would be nearly impossible to get anything accomplished. He wouldn't be at the top of his game, and then what use would he be to the clan if he couldn't perform his duties?

"I need some air." Styx turned on his heels and headed toward the door. He wouldn't go far, but he needed to think without having her scent tainting his mind.

"Styx…" Mira called to him as he opened the door.

"Why don't you give him a few minutes?" Theodore suggested.

With a slight nod, she pulled the blanket tighter around her. "I'm sorry."

He wanted to tell her that it wasn't her fault, it was his, but the words wouldn't come. He had just begun to accept his past, and how it brought him to where he needed to be, but now that everything was changing again it was throwing his progress to the wind. He wasn't worthy of her, or any mate for that matter. There was too much blood on his hands, some of it the blood of innocents. A man like that didn't deserve happiness—or the love of a good woman.

Chapter Seven

Mira paced the inside of the small cabin, and with every minute that passed her beast became more on edge. The tigress within didn't like being separated from the man that was supposed to be her mate, not with the bond incomplete. She was even more on edge because he seemed to be upset that they were to be mated. At first, she might have been appalled that she was to be his mate, and it was true that originally she would not have chosen him, but that had begun to change. She had seen a different side of him, one that was gentle, and she wanted to explore that. Even with her worst doubts, her beast didn't seem to care about his past. It only wanted the mating.

She'd rather she had more time to get to know him before she was pushed into cementing the bond, yet she'd do what she needed to. There was a question that floated through her thoughts that she didn't want to face. *Am I willing to leave my clan?* If David had taken over the clan, what did it mean for them? Would she be welcomed back, or would he reject her since he had worked so closely with Frank?

Mating with Styx would mean she wasn't just starting her life over, or just with him, but also with a whole new clan. She was a supporter, but she'd have to find a way to give more to the Alaskan Tigers. Did she even have a skill that was worthy of them? Frank had kept most of the clan submissive, crushing all their desires. He'd give them jobs they hated so they wouldn't be overly successful. He never wanted anyone growing so much that he'd have to squash them down again. *He made sure all of us were thoroughly squashed.*

"I'm not sure who's more conflicted, you or him."

She paused and found Theodore reclined on the sofa, his head resting against the pillows, but his eyes on her. "The rollercoaster ride of life," she retorted.

"You've been pacing for twenty minutes. Have you come to any decisions yet?"

"Decisions on what? I'm not the one who just walked out of here."

"Raja's words cut deep for Styx. He's duty oriented, and the idea of not being able to perform his duties is a hard pill to swallow."

She stopped pacing and came to sit on the chair next to the sofa. "I'm *not* a duty."

"You're right. He might have come here out of duty, but you're his mate. Nonetheless, that wasn't what I meant." He adjusted so he could get a better look at her. "I meant that he doesn't like the idea that he's pressured into this mating in order to continue doing the only thing that he's devoted his life to protecting Tabitha and the Elders. He's strong enough to be an Alpha of his own clan, but he won't do it."

"I asked him about that, and he said it was because no one would follow him due to his past."

"That's his excuse, but it's because he enjoys what he does. He's a protector. The idea of him stepping into the position of Alpha, and then having people protect him instead isn't something he would take well to. He would rather protect the people close to him than have them risk themselves," he explained. "But there's something else about him that you're missing."

"What?" She had never been around other species before, and wasn't really sure what to make of the bear before her but he was starting to grow on her.

"He feels he doesn't deserve you." He scooted up to lean against the pillows. "Frank used twisted stories about Styx to scare your clan, but it was Styx who earned that reputation. He spent many years as an assassin, and the blood on his hands is thicker than most. While he might have left that life behind, he's still an Elder guard and that means spilling blood occasionally. He believes you should be mated to someone who's better suited to you."

"Better suited to me? What's that supposed to mean?"

"Styx has been soft with you so far, doing what he can to make you feel comfortable and hiding the worst of himself from you, but once the mating bond is intact, there's nothing he can do to stop you from seeing everything. To have his mate shun him because of what he's done, and who he's become because of that, would break him. He's a strong man, but to be denied the mate he had finally found due to the past that lead him to her could turn him rogue. When you agree to the mating, you need to be sure you're ready."

"There's no way out of mating other than through death," she reminded him.

"True, but there are ways to make your mate miserable, and if he was rogue that could break the connection as well. He would no longer be Styx, he'd just be the beast that normally lies within us." He met her gaze. "You must be willing to accept him, all of him, because with that first rush of the mating bond, you'll know everything about him. Possibly more than you ever wanted to know."

"What if I learn something I can't accept?"

"When that rush happens, don't focus on the past, but focus on the now. Know that everything that happened brought him to you. He would lay down his life for a cause he believes in, and that's the future of shifters. Because of those skills he learned as an assassin, he's now able to defend the Elders of the Alaskan Tigers. Those were the same qualities that made Ty send him after you. There's no one in the world that could fight for you like he will. Never doubt that the man is so much more than a former assassin or a guard. He's not just a fighter."

"What is he?"

Theodore shot her an all-knowing smirk. "That, Mira, you'll need to learn for yourself."

"Then it's time to find out." She tossed her blanket on the arm of the chair and headed for the door. "I'm going to find him."

"I think it might be best to let him have sometime before…"

"It's time I find out who I'm to be mated with. If this is going to work, it's time we're both open and honest with each other. It's also time I find out why he's under this notion that he's not worthy of mating."

"I wish you luck, because to get through to him you're going to need it." Theodore smirked. "I'm going to try to sleep."

"I've a feeling I need more than luck." She closed the door behind her and stepped out into the cold night air. Snow blew through the air in big thick flakes. She scanned the ground, but as far as she could see there was no one moving about in the darkness, not that she was surprised due to the late hour. She couldn't even see guards, but then she had learned that the compound was large with over nine hundred and fifty acres, so the perimeter guards were probably far off in the distance.

Searching for Styx, she sniffed the air and was met with the scent of crisp wood burning in various cabin fireplaces. She'd give anything to be curled up in front of the fire, instead of out in the winter night. Whatever the issue was between them, they had to get over it and quickly. The longer it went on, the more the mating connection would grow. Already, the tingling was increasing within her, and soon that would become a painful burning.

She wasn't sure about this whole mating situation, nor was she convinced he was the right one for her, but they'd have to find a way to make it work because death for either of them wasn't an option. She strolled farther into the darkness, toward where she sensed him, and tried to remember she was safe within a compound. *Mated forever to a former assassin.*

If the powers that be had thought this mating through, they'd have given him someone with more spunk. Someone who could save herself, not be cannon fodder. Since Frank had beaten the will out of the clan, that's what she was. She hadn't been raised to have a backbone. Even in the privacy of their one room, there had never been any resistance, not from her, her siblings, or even her parents. Everyone fell in line with what their Alpha ordered. The first sign of resistance she had shown was her support of Tabitha and the future she was trying to bring and even that had been hidden deep within. The only exception being that she'd told her sister. *Look where that got me. Next time I'll keep my mouth shut.*

"You shouldn't be out here." Styx's deep voice drifted toward her just as he stepped out of the woods and headed directly for her.

"I've come to find you." Her beast perked up at the sight of him, and she took a deep breath as if to wrap herself in the aroma of him. The deep evergreen scent with fresh rain and crisp…apples. It was the apples that threw her off, but she was certain of it now. Earlier, she hadn't known what the sweet, slightly fruity scent was, but now she had no doubt.

"I'd have come back in a bit. There was nothing that should have brought you out here."

"You brought me out here." She closed the distance between them until she was only a few steps before him. "Why do you look at me like that?"

"Like what?" He clasped one hand over his opposite wrist and watched her.

"You look at me like you want me, but at the same time as if you want to run. What about me makes you so appalled?"

"You think this is about you." A deep chuckle sent a sparkle of glee to his eyes.

"You don't want to be mated to me, and I get that. I'm not strong, or a fighter, but unless you're willing to kill me, then we're stuck with each other. I'm sure as hell not going to commit suicide just to make your life easier, and I don't have the skills to kill you even if I wanted to."

"It's just like a woman to think they have it all figured out." He shook his head. "Catnip, you have no idea what you're talking about."

"Really?" She tipped her head to the side in question. "I think I see it quite clearly. You're not happy with this mating, which is fine because I'm not sure how I feel, either, but we're going to have to deal with that."

"How do you suggest we deal with it?"

"I suggest you start by explaining why you seem to despise me."

"I don't, and if that's what you think, you're not looking closely enough. Either that or your misreading the situation." He nodded to the bench. "We won't get any privacy in the cabin so why don't we sit and talk."

"I hope if I'm going to sit out here in the freezing cold and the snow you're going to tell me what's going on with you." She strolled forward and took a seat on the bench.

"If you think this is cold, wait until you get to Alaska," he teased and sat beside her.

"So?" she questioned when he didn't make a move to tell her what the issue was.

"I spent more than half my life as an assassin, and have only begun to atone for the blood on my hands since I've become a part of the Alaskan Tigers. I've been promoted from a perimeter guard to one of the Elder guards, but it's still not enough. Have I tried to change people's opinion of me? No, because it keeps the Elders safe and that's my goal. I have much that I still haven't accepted in my past, so how can I expect my mate to accept those things? I expected more time to atone for what I've done before mating, so that my mate would be able to see the changes in me. Most just see me as a cold-blooded killer that I take someone's life without emotion, but it's not true."

"Since we're being honest, I'll admit that you scared the ever-living hell out of me when I found out who you were."

He smirked at her. "I remember. I thought I'd have to knock you unconscious to get you onto the plane. That would have just been another thing we'd have to overcome to make this work between us."

"I'm not saying it's going to be easy, but I think we can do it." She reached out and placed her hand over his. "Maybe it's this mating bond between us, but to me you're a different man than you were before. Coming to my rescue proved that. The point is, I'm not terrified of you like I was before. Am I thrilled with your past? Maybe not, but our past brought us to where we are. It would've been easier to keep quiet about my support for Tabitha. But then I wouldn't have been here, and I wouldn't have found you."

"Our past and our decisions brought us here, but once the mating is cemented, you'll know how grizzly my past is."

"But I'll also know the man you are now, and the man before me matters more than the person you once were."

He scooted closer and put his arm around her shoulders. "Here's to a future of brighter tomorrows and less looking into the darkened past."

They sat there in silence for a moment, and she realized they had overcome something. It was the first hurdle, but it was something, and there was an ease between them now. "Styx…" She tipped her head up to look at him, her cheek brushing against the thin material of his shirt. "I need…I need to see them. I need to see David and anyone else who survived."

"I was afraid of that."

"Afraid of that, why? Do you think he'd call me back into a trap?"

"It's possible it could be a trap, but if we're going to go, we'll make sure we're prepared."

"What do you mean *if* we go? I told you I need to go."

"But the question is, can you handle what you might find there?" He adjusted to look at her but kept his arm firmly around her. "We know David survived and there must be some others who survived, otherwise he wouldn't have claimed Alpha status, but we don't know if any of your other family members or friends survived. Going and finding out that most or all of them are dead is going to be a shock, and you're going to want to grieve but we can't show any weakness."

"I am a weakness."

"Catnip, you've got more fight in you than you give yourself credit for. You survived for days on your own. Your spirit has been broken, but you're not weak. The sense of freedom you have now is sparking the tigress within you to rise. The beast won't be stifled easily this time." He tangled his hand into her hair, his fingertips brushed against her scalp. "I'm going to help you regain your sense of freedom. No one will ever hurt you again."

"I don't want you to do it out of some misplaced duty." She was tempted to pull back from him to prove her point but it wasn't just the beast that had been stifled before, it was also the woman within and in that moment she wanted to be free. She wanted to feel his caresses and embraces, even if it was just because of the mating bond, and not out of love.

"You're not a duty. You're my mate."

"Then I guess there's only one thing left to do."

"If we're going to Connecticut, I guess there is." He let out a deep sigh.

His gaze left hers and went skyward, but something about it let her know that he wasn't seeing the stars overhead that lit the night sky. Somehow, the decision to accept this mating had added distance between them again. Only, this time, she wasn't sure what caused it. "Styx…"

"Come on." He rose from the bench and started toward the edge of the trees. "We can't do this at the cabin unless you want to kick out Theodore, but I know of a place."

With little choice but to follow him if she wanted to move past this current bump, she rose from the bench and followed after him. "I don't think I understand you. One minute I think we moved past this wall that you use to shut everyone out, and the next you've done it again. What was that sigh for? There was a look in your eyes that screamed you'd rather be miles away than do what we're about to do."

"Conflicting emotions." He didn't even bother to turn around when he answered her, he just kept his pace as they made their way between the trees.

"I know that feeling, but aren't we supposed to be in this together?" She stopped dead in her tracks. "Damn it, Styx, this is hard for me too, and I'm getting a little tired of the mood swings coming from you. One minute you seem content with this mating and the next you're pushing me away. It's throwing me off balance and I don't know if I'm coming or going."

"I have a feeling it's only going to get worse as the night progresses." He stopped but didn't turn back to look at her.

"You're not unworthy."

"What?" He spun around to look at her and even in the darkness she could see his body tighten.

"Theodore said you believe you're unworthy of mating because of your past." She crossed the space between them and came to stand just before him. "You're not."

"That bear talks too much."

"He's enlightening." She smirked. "I'm being truthful. You're not unworthy of this."

"I've stolen the last breaths of more people than I care to count. I've left widowed mates in my wake and for what? The excuse that I thought I was delivering justice only goes so far, especially when you consider how most of the kills were based on lies. My former Alpha deceived me and many others, but I didn't realize the lies until it was too late."

"You know the number."

"What?"

"Don't stand there and tell me that you don't know the number of people you killed because you do." She reached out and placed her hand over his bicep. "Every single time you've killed, it's stayed with you."

"How do you know this?" His voice was rough but he didn't pull away from her.

"This bond between us is overwhelming, and most of it I can't make sense of yet because it's so jumbled, but this I know with undying certainty. You have conflicting emotions because you haven't accepted your past." There was a sadness in his eyes that let her know that she was speaking the truth. "But there's a part within you that wants this mating, and it's not just the tiger urging you on. Focus on that."

"Catnip, you have no idea what you're getting yourself into it."

"I'm not going to be appalled by what the connection shows me. You're more than the man of your past, and I'll remember that. But have you considered the fact you might not be pleased with me, or what you see during the bonding?"

"There's nothing that I could see that would change this." He uncrossed his arms from his chest, and placed his hands on her hips.

"I'm not the strong woman you need by your side, but I'll try."

"You don't see yourself in the same way I see you. It took courage to run, to keep Frank's men off your trail, and to stay alive while you were waiting for us. That's strength." He stared down at her for a moment before he added, "You have no idea what you're getting into—"

She interrupted him by shaking her head. "Not that again."

"I'm not talking about mating with me. I mean by supporting Tabitha and coming back to Alaska with me. It's dangerous, and we have many more battles before us."

"With you on the frontlines."

"It's my duty, but more than that I do it because I know what the world will be like when Tabitha has completely claimed her place and everyone follows her."

"How much opposition is there?" Talking about him being on the frontlines of their future sent a chill of fear through her. How much danger would her mate be in?

He glanced around the woods, and even as he did so, she let her beast come a little closer to the surface to get a better idea of their surroundings. Was there something that sparked his interest in the darkness? She couldn't smell anything other than the woods and fireplaces.

"Not here." He turned and kept his arm around her. "There's a small guard cabin not far from here. It's vacant since Jinx bought additional land a few years ago and expanded the perimeter. We'll have privacy there."

She leaned close to him. Anyone who was watching would have thought they were just two lovebirds, but she did it to keep her question from being overheard. "Is there someone watching?"

"There's no one nearby, and even if there was, this clan is our ally. There's just no use standing out here in the cold any longer."

She let him lead her toward the cabin, while she scanned the darkness.

There was no doubt her mind that he was always on alert, and if there was any danger in the area he would have already reacted to it. Nevertheless, something had changed. It was subtle, but it was there. Were there more enemies to Tabitha's regime than he wanted to admit?

Chapter Eight

There was a thin layer of dust over every surface, making it clear the cabin had not been used in a while, but at least they were sheltered from the cold wind. The inside was bare except for an old table without any chairs and a bed. Even though they had been in bed together before, it had been innocent. Now, the bed against the back wall seemed to scream their intentions. Mira sat down on the edge of the bed, rubbing her hand against the thin plaid comforter.

"There's opposition just as there would be with any change." He stood near the window and watched her. "As time goes on, they'll see what is happening is for the best. Otherwise, we'll have to deal with them."

"Deal with them, as in kill them?"

"There are other alternatives to killing them. We'll try to reason with them first. In the end it will be their decision. We can't leave someone in power who is opposed to us, otherwise all the good that Tabitha and Ty are doing will be for nothing. Does that bother you to know I might kill again?"

She met his gaze and shook her head. "No. Maybe it should, but it doesn't. I know the reasoning for it, and if you can take an Alpha like Frank out of his position of power, then I don't care how you do it, just that it's done. The clans who have Alphas like him need to be free. Hopefully, it won't cost them the same price I paid."

He cleared his throat. "I know you want to go to Connecticut, but I think we need to call your brother in the morning and see where things stand before we fly out."

"Why? So you have more time to adjust to this mating?"

"This mating has nothing to do with it. I want to make sure it's safe enough for you to return. Frank has ruled for years, breaking the will of every clan member until there was no fight left within them. There are bound to be supporters within the clan, and if David hasn't gained control of them it will be dangerous for you. They'll see you as the final task Frank wanted complete and will seek to eliminate you. I'm not going to take the risk just so you can see your brother." He crossed the small space to kneel before her. "I know you want to go, but I won't risk you. He might need time to gain control over the clan before you can visit."

"Are you just doing this so that we don't have to complete our mating tonight?"

"No. I'm still planning on doing that. It will put us on solid ground, and we'll know where we stand with each other. Otherwise, we're going to continue to have this war of emotions raging within us. I don't know about you, but I'm tired of it."

She was beyond tired of it. She felt as though every time she got her bearings, something slammed against her, knocking her off-balance again. The mating might help, but she also suspected it would give her yet another wave of uncertainties. They were being forced together, but it wasn't out of love. It was very much the same as arranged marriages. Only she wasn't sure the two of them could ever have the relationships she'd witnessed with other mates. Would they ever fall in love with each other? Or would it always be the connection of their beasts that kept them together?

When Styx referred to the ups and downs as a war of raging emotions, he wasn't underestimating it. That's what it felt like. Every time he thought he had things under control, his thoughts would carry him away again, back into the past, bringing a new wave of doubts before him. If she was to be his, then she'd have to accept what he came from, and the only way to do that was for her to see it for herself.

"Are you ready?"

"As ready as I'm going to be." She started to tug up her sweater, but he placed his hand over hers, stopping her.

"You're nervous. Just take a deep breath and let it out. Let your tigress lead the way and stop thinking like a human. If we're heading to Connecticut soon, we don't have time to get to know each other better and take our time to come to this point. We've got to take the leap of faith, and know that it will be better on the other side."

She did as he asked, and after a few deep breaths her body began to relax. He wrapped his hand around her wrist and pulled her up until she was standing before him, the fronts of their bodies touching. "We're going to take it slow, and if you want to stop just say so. This is somewhat an unusual mating, what with the rush, so we need to trust in our destinies and our tigers."

"What lies in my future couldn't be worse than where I've come from."

He hoped that was true but a vindictive Alpha might have been more doable than what she will see in his past once the mating bond has formed. With a vindictive Alpha there were ways around that and ways to stay out of his path of torture. On the other hand with a mate she was stuck with him. Even if she was appalled by what she saw within him, her beast wouldn't give up what was between them.

"Don't look at me like you're expecting me to run screaming from the room." She placed her hand on his arm, just above the elbow. "We both have things from our past that we're not proud of, but we'll get through it. It's not like we have a choice."

"Just because the mating bond would be in place, it doesn't mean it would be a happy mating. You could despise me and not be able to stand the sight of me. That would be worse…" He stopped himself before he could finish. It might be worse than anything he'd encountered in his past, but he wasn't willing to show how much he wanted someone to accept him. Not even to his mate.

"Let's get this over with."

He didn't like the sound of that, as if she had already decided this wasn't going to work, but he was willing to risk the mating bond in order to get her back to her brother and clan. "If you want to go home, maybe the distance will keep the pain from the denied mating away."

"Second thoughts? You know the distance won't help, and the first twinges of pain from this mating can already be felt. The longer we put this off, the worse it will be." She raised an eyebrow at him in question. "Or is the assassin afraid of what he might find hidden behind the shell of his mate?"

"No." His tone was harsher than he intended because of the way she taunted him with the word *assassin*. It was his former life, something he wasn't proud of, and he didn't want to be reminded of it.

"We're both exhausted, so we need to do this."

He stopped hesitating and threw caution to the wind. *Mate or suffer the consequences.* Slowly, he slid his hand up her arm and watched as the heat from the simple touch brought the change in her eyes. Her tigress edged closer to the surface, lighting the orangey glow within her eyes, and turning the smoky blue into a fiery orange.

He cupped the back of her head, tangling his fingers into the long strands of her hair, and leaned in for a kiss. His lips gently brushed against the softness of hers. The sweet spiciness met him, urging him forward. He kissed her again, this time with more passion, and she met his desire with that of her own. His tongue slipped between her lips before teasing along the sharpness of her teeth.

With each kiss, their desire grew. A soft moan escaped her and she pressed herself closer to him, sliding her hand up his body. All hesitation disappeared as their tigers led the way to their destinies.

He pulled back, ending the kiss, and leaving them both breathless for a moment. Their gazes locked and no longer did the fear shine in her eyes, which were now full of desire and need. "Styx…don't stop."

"Have no fear, Catnip." He took hold of the edge of her sweater and pulled it over her head. Curves in all the right places sparked another wave of desire within him and he ran his hands along her hips until he reached just below her bra. "Take this off and lie back."

Arching her back, her breasts pressed against his chest, as she reached behind her and unhooked the bra. "I'm not sure it's fair I'm this naked while you're still fully dressed."

"Shh, I'm trying to put you at ease." When she didn't lie back he stepped toward her, forcing her back onto the bed.

"I'm not nervous any longer. I want the essences of our beasts to mingle together and bond. I want you, Styx."

"That is the mating desire talking." He climbed onto the bed beside her, teasing his hand up the side of her chest.

"No, it's me. I was terrified before. Some of that is because of what I've been brainwashed with, but the rest of that is because everything is so upside down in my life. I'm alone. Even if David has gained control over the clan, it will never be my home again. Too many risks there, since my so-called betrayal was what got many of my former clan family killed. I'd never be safe there."

"That's why you're returning to Alaska with me."

"What am I supposed to do there? I've no skills."

"Catnip, you continue to underestimate yourself, but I'm going to prove to you that you're so much more. You'll come home with me and be a part of what you were willing to risk everything for. The future will be amazing and you're going to play a role in bringing it around." His fingers teased over her nipple, gently rolling it between his forefinger and thumb. "Now, enough talk, I've got something better to do with my mouth."

He pressed himself along the length of her body, and his tongue teased around her areola before sliding over the nipple. He dragged his teeth over the area, sending a wave of chills through her and making her arch her back toward him, thrusting more of her breast to his mouth. His fingers teased her other nipple until it stood to attention.

"You're beautiful." He slid his hand down her stomach, his finger circling around her bellybutton before moving to the top button of her jeans. "Are you still okay with this?" He paused, not moving toward the zipper as he waited for her answer.

"Yes." Her voice was breathy with need.

With that, he slid the zipper down and tugged her jeans over her hips. She kicked off her shoes, making it easier for him to slide them off the rest of the way. She was naked before him, and his beast surged forward.

He crushed his mouth to hers and slid his hand between her legs. His fingers slipped between her folds, quickly finding her center. The simple touch pulled a moan from deep within her. He slid a finger within her while his thumb made contact with her clit, gently rubbing over it. She pushed against his hand, and with one final kiss he pulled back so he could watch as her body responded to his touch.

The beauty of mating wasn't just that they'd have someone to spend their lives with, it was the way they were supposed to be completely matched. The way her body responded to him, the moans of pleasure, and the glaze to her eyes, were all undeniable signs that they were meant to be together. With every wiggle and push against him, he sped his pace, letting his finger slide in and out of her while continuing to caress her clit with his thumb. With every moan, he grew in confidence when it came to her. They'd find a way to work through all the other drama because this was what mating was all about.

The way she moaned his name had him wanting to remove his hand and shove another part of him deep within her core. Still, he held off. He scooted lower on the bed, spread her legs, and lowered his head. The instant his tongue traced along the tip of her clit, she gasped. Enjoying the way her body reacted, he licked over the sensitive bud, sucking it gently. She tried to wiggle away, but he held tight to her hips, keeping her just where he wanted her. Over and over he licked, until her body was taut and ready for her release.

Another moan had fierce desire rising within him, and he wanted to take her right then. This slow pace would work better without the mating desire burning within them. He needed her now.

"Styx." She took hold of his shirt and tugged it up his chest. Her nails grazing along his back as she did so. "I want you naked."

He let her slide his shirt over his head before he rose off the bed and stripped off the rest of his clothes. His shaft was already hard as he stepped out of his jeans and boxers and moved to the bed.

"Come here." She rose up and scooted to the edge of the bed. "Now I want to taste you." She leaned forward, kissing the tip of him before letting him slip between her lips. Taking him into her mouth, her hand worked at the base and he tangled his hand in the strands of her hair, holding her close. Her mouth worked up and down the length of him, milking him.

He moaned her name before placing a hand on her shoulder. "Not like this. I want to be inside you, and with the mating bond so close, I won't last long."

She let him slip from her mouth and he climbed back onto the bed next to her. He kissed her neck, nibbling down her jawline to her shoulder. He wrapped his mouth around her nipple, flicking his tongue over the bud, drawing it to full hardness. He teased over to the other one, tweaking it until it stood at attention. A moan of ecstasy echoed through the cabin when his tongue flicked over one hardened tip.

"Styx." Her voice cracked with desire.

He let her nipple slip from between his lips as he gazed up at her. "Yes, Catnip?" His eyes gleamed and his lips curved up into the cocky smile she had come to know was all him. He grabbed her hips and pulled her so she was straddling him.

"Don't make me beg for what I need." Soft purrs mixed within her words. "You told me to embrace my tigress, but she's impatient."

He caressed his way up from her hips, sending moans of ecstasy from her lips. Heat soared through his blood, like a fire burning just below the skin, impatient and demanding. As she straddled him, he leaned up to kiss a path down her neck, his thumb playing over her nipple. Sensations collided and threatened to overwhelm her when he teased her nipples. She wiggled her hips, his shaft rubbing against her folds. "Please, I want you."

With every touch, she arched against him, demanding more. Within him his beast roared with frustration and need, but he swatted it down again. If this was the only time he had his mate without the fear of him in her eyes, he'd take his time. Next time they were together might only be to satisfy the mating desire, and not because they wanted to. He kissed along her throat, his teeth grazing over her skin, only to be met with a demanding moan vibrating in her throat.

"Styx…" She cried out as her hand wrapped around his shaft. "Now! Or I'll make you suffer."

"Oh my, the kitty has found her claws." He spread her legs farther, giving him the access he needed. His shaft slid along her folds, and his control snapped. Instead of being gentle and easing his way into her, as he had planned. He pushed himself in, thrusting himself completely inside her.

He buried himself deep within her, only to pull out and slam back in again. With each thrust he sped his pace, each time completely filling her with his manhood. The heat between them built and their beasts mingled, amping up the tension building within him. Every glide of his shaft inside her seemed to set off another cascade of heat. Their bodies rocked back and forth, tension stretching her tighter as they fought for the release they longed for.

"Faster." She clenched her muscles tightly around him and her nails dragged along his chest.

He grabbed hold of her hips, and as he plunged toward her, he pushed her down onto him. Together they worked to find the rhythm they needed until their breaths grew ragged as he rocked in and out of her. Each thrust brought him closer to the ecstasy he longed for.

"Oh, Styx." She tipped her head back and cried out his name as her release took hold. Her nails dragged down his chest, drawing blood, but he didn't care. His own orgasm followed. As he buried himself inside of her one last time, he tipped his head back and roared.

Mine...

Chapter Nine

With the mating bond firmly intact, Mira laid curled next to Styx and tried to make sense of everything she felt. He expected her to be appalled by his past, but she wasn't. The blood of those he killed roiled her stomach, but not because of his actions. The blood only reminded her of all the blood Frank had spilled over the years. While it was true that he was an assassin and had more kills than anyone else, she had seen what had brought him to that. It wasn't out of the desire to kill and he wasn't a sociopath looking for an easy way to get away with murder. Like her, he had been led astray by someone he trusted. Lies led him to kill because he thought he was saving the world from a scumbag.

She also knew something that no one else knew. *Sasha.* She tipped her head up to him and found him watching her as if waiting for her to pull away from him. "I'm so sorry."

"What for?"

"Sasha." The name rolled off her tongue like a lead weight and her stomach sank. She was about to fall neck deep into murky waters.

"That was long ago."

The words didn't match with his reaction. His body tightened and his eyes filled with pain. Years might have passed on the calendar, but to him it was still a wound he carried within him. Never quite healing, only being bandaged over. No matter how he tried, the death of his sister was always there.

"I know what I feel, and maybe I know parts of it, but with everything flooding toward me at once I can't keep things straight. What happened?" She ran her hand along his chest and hugged herself tighter to him.

"She's dead, what more matters?"

"It matters because she's the reason you became an assassin. You tried to protect her." His pain ripped through her as if it was her own. "You've never shared the story with anyone but it's time you tell it. Tell me."

He closed his eyes and leaned back against the pillows. "Sasha was a wild child. Maybe it was growing up on the streets and having to fend for ourselves, but she rebelled and got into some deep shit. We were in New York and there was a group of underground shifters. They weren't of any one animal group, more like rebels joined together to survive. Sasha started hanging around with them, even began to experiment with drugs. Because of the beast within, things don't affect us the same way as humans, so she was doing more and more of the drugs trying to seek that high she so badly wanted. It became expensive quickly and she couldn't pay the shifter she owed money to. He was the leader of the group and threatened to kill her if she didn't pay up."

"You offered to work off her debt in exchange for her life," she supplied when he fell silent.

"What else was I supposed to do, see her be murdered? I was her older brother and it was my job to watch out for her. In the end, I failed."

She laced her fingers around his. "You didn't fail. You saved her then, and you would have saved her later if you had known."

"If you already know this, why are you making me tell you?"

"You need to get it off your chest. Who better to share the pain with than your mate? Now, go on."

"I didn't know what I was getting myself into when I agreed to work off her debt. It started small, with guard duties and some minor unwanted tasks, but nothing I couldn't handle. I thought I was getting off easy. Sasha was clean…it only lasted a few weeks, but it was something. When she started doing the drugs again, that's when everything changed. No longer was he satisfied with what I was doing, and I received my first target." He let out a deep sigh that held so much regret. "If I refused, Sasha's life would be forfeited. He even held her hostage until the hit was complete to ensure I didn't try to whisk her away to safety."

"That was the first step to you becoming an assassin."

"Yes." He opened his eyes and their gazes met. "When she died, I embraced the job because of my anger. I had hoped that eliminating another scumbag would help me move past my own grief, but it didn't. Instead, I just buried it deep within."

"I know she killed herself, but why? Was she able to find the right combination of drugs that worked for her?" She tried to approach the subject carefully, but she wanted to know.

He shook his head. "She was to be mated, and the tiger was worse than any we had met before. What she didn't know was he was my next hit. I was hunting him when she took her own life. She left me a note explaining that she'd rather be dead than be trapped with him. If only I had known that was her destiny, I could have told her he'd be dead before he could even lay a paw on her." His voice trailed off, and he laid there for a few minutes before adding, "After she started using, we started to grow apart. I didn't know what to do for her and every time I tried to fix her, it seemed to make things worse. The gap between us grew until we came to a point where we stopped confiding in each other. That's when we doomed ourselves."

"I'm sorry." She rose up on her elbow, so she could get a better view of him. "Her choices were her own, and in the end it led her to an early grave. Those choices also took you down a road that led you to me. I'm sorry for your loss, for the pain you've suffered, but I'm not sorry it brought us together."

"For the first time, I don't regret it either. My past was the reason I was sent after you. Ty and Tabitha knew I was the best chance you had, especially since you went to Washington D.C. My years as an assassin make others think twice before they screw with me. It makes me good at what I do now, and keeps those I'm in charge of protecting safe. It will keep you safe, too."

"Even if your past was different, you'd still keep me safe. You saved me when I needed it the most and you made me feel like I belonged again. When I left my clan, I lost that scene of belonging, but you brought it back to me."

"We brought it back to each other. Though I have belonged to the Alaskan Tigers for some time now, you gave me back what I've been missing since Sasha died. I'll admit I was terrified that you would turn from me, and this bond. Yet, here you are."

"And I'm not going anywhere. You're stuck with me."

"There's no one else I'd rather be stuck with." He wrapped his arms tightly around her. "We should try to get some sleep. In a few hours, we can call David and make our decisions."

She nodded and snuggled deeper into his embrace. An hour ago, she felt no connection to him. He still had her on edge, but that all changed. She wouldn't say she was in love with him, but there was a bond between them that made her willing to stand up and fight for him. She wasn't lying when she said she wasn't going anywhere. They were meant to be, and there had to be a reason destiny had decided to tie them together for all eternity. *Mated to heal each other and make us into a stronger pair.*

Morning came long before Styx was ready for it. He would've preferred a few more hours alone with his mate, cuddled together while the world passed them

100

by. He didn't want to get out of bed and call David, because no matter what news he had for her, it would bring the sadness back. He had no doubt that there were at least some deaths that David would report that would hit home for her. By mid-day, they'd know just how many friends and relatives she had lost and how much damage Frank managed to do to the clan before his death.

In a little more than twenty-four hours, his whole life had changed. He went from being alone, with no one understanding him, to being mated. It was all a whirlwind. He suspected the next day or two were going to be more so. His mate was going to go through many emotions as she accepted what had happened to her sister and other clan members. It pained him that the only thing he could do was be there for her, even when she fought against him. And she would, because her decisions brought her to him.

He rubbed his cheek along the side of her face, her hairs teasing along his skin as he marked her again. "Catnip."

"Huh?" Her voice was whisper quiet and she barely stirred.

"We should get up."

"Just a bit longer." She tugged the thin blanket closer to her chin.

"I wouldn't wake you if it wasn't important." He brushed the hair away from her face and stared down at her. She was beautiful, her face soft and relaxed as she fought to cling to sleep. "We need to call David and make a decision if we're going there or back to Alaska."

A soft growl answered him and her eyelids popped open. "Fine, but I need some *strong* coffee first."

"I'm sure Theodore has some made and waiting for us." To keep himself from claiming her again, he forced himself out of bed and began dressing.

"I've been thinking…" She leaned back on the pillows. "I think I should go alone."

"What?" There was no doubt she meant to Connecticut, and he wasn't letting that happen.

"Frank instilled fear in the members when it came to you. If you show up, they're going to think you're there to kill them," she reasoned.

"It won't be the first time someone thought that, and I suspect it won't be the last either." He slipped his shirt over his head. "The fear they have when it comes to me will keep you safe."

"I don't want them to be scared of me. Some of them are my family…my friends."

"And some of them are your enemies. They might seek to kill you because of what happened and in revenge for the people who died. I'm not letting that happen." Now dressed, he grabbed her clothes from the floor where they were tossed hours before and held them out to her. "We haven't even decided it's safe for you to go. We need to call David and see where things stand first."

"If my brother asks me to come, I can't deny him."

"He took over the clan, but he's not your Alpha. No matter the status of the clan, or where he stands on supporting Tabitha, he can't be your Alpha. You must return to Alaska with me."

She snatched her clothes from him. "Controlling me, just like Frank did."

"Catnip…" He raised an eyebrow at her as if letting her know she wasn't thinking clearly.

"Don't *Catnip* me!" she snapped.

"I'm only telling you what must happen. You knew it when you agreed to this mating. My duty lies in Alaska, and to the Elders of the clan. I must return and you will be at my side." He had thought she would have wanted to go to Alaska. After all, she called them to rescue her, and it seemed like the ultimate outcome of the whole situation.

"You think you've got it all figured out, and that I'll just follow you. Maybe David needs me. Maybe I can help my clan."

"They're not your clan any longer." He took a deep breath and tried not to give into his tiger's irritation. "David couldn't protect you from the clan members. It would be seen as showing favoritism. If they'd challenge you, you'd have no choice but to accept, and David could do nothing. It would be their right because of the role you played in the demise of the clan. If you commit to David as your Alpha, it could mean your death. You must see that."

"So, returning to Alaska with you is my only way of surviving." She fastened her bra and pulled the sweater over her head before moving to the edge of the bed to finish dressing.

"It must have been what you wanted." He reached down and touched her shoulder. "You can commit to Ty, serve the clan to make sure that Tabitha can complete her destiny, and be with me. What's holding you back from that?" He waited, even as his tiger fought against her emotions.

"In truth…fear." Her lips curled down into a frown and her shoulders sank. "Fear of the unknown."

He took hold of her hand and pulled her up into his arms. "It's normal but I'm going to be there every step of the way. I promise you're going to fit into the clan and in no time it will be your home."

"What if it's not? Then I'm stuck."

"You have my word that it's going to be fine." There was nothing that could be said or done to relieve her apprehension. "The sooner we get to Alaska, the sooner you'll realize this. The longer we take here, or in Connecticut, will only increase your uneasiness."

"I know you're not lying. I can feel the truth between our beasts, but it doesn't eliminate my nervousness." She wrapped her arms around his waist. "I've never been away from the clan. I can count on one hand how many times I left the compound. One of those rare times was the trip to Washington D.C. It's why I went there, thinking the crowd would help keep me safe. Frank controlled every aspect of our lives. This freedom is…unnerving."

"I know, Catnip, but things will be okay. You're going to enjoy this new freedom. I've no doubt that Tabitha, Bethany, Kallie, Robin, Courtney, and the other females of the clan will look out for you, and have you enjoying life in no time. Now, get dressed and we can find out what we're going to do."

"As much as I'm nervous about going to Alaska, I'm excited. I believe in what Tabitha and all of you are doing. I want to be a part of that, but I'm not sure what I can do that will be helpful."

"We'll work it out." He kissed her forehead before she stepped back to dress.

What was happening between them was quicker than he might be comfortable with, but he didn't have time to give into his own unease. He needed to be strong and reassuring for her. They'd get this over with quickly, and get her back to his clan to help ease the doubt. It would also give them time to get to know each other better, to connect on another level. Their time alone wouldn't just be getting to know each other's personalities, but also he had plans to explore more of her body.

Mira's heart beat frantically against her ribcage, in such a way she wouldn't have been surprised if there were bruises to match its pattern. Thump, thump, over and over again. Her vision swam before her eyes, as her anxiety level flew off the chart.

"It's okay. He can't hurt you." Styx rubbed a hand along her back.

"I've never been afraid of David, even as he grew in power to be Frank's…I guess *assistant* is the best word. Frank would have never trusted anyone for the position of Lieutenant. He was Frank's toy, someone who did what Frank didn't want to do himself, and was used as an extra set of eyes watching the clan. But it was never a position of a trusted advisor or anything like that. There wasn't even a true friendship bond between them, now that I really think of it."

"Why did he take the position, then?" Theodore stood on the other side of the small kitchen counter, coffee mug in hand.

"Frank ordered it. He wanted it, and even though David was happy with his position within the clan, it was either he did it or it would have been his death. He did it to protect the family and stay alive. Dad's health was starting to fail, and he felt it was his duty to keep us safe. He told Frank he'd do it if he left our family alone."

"Your Alpha agreed to that?" Theodore set the mug aside and stepped closer to them. "It doesn't sound like Frank would be willing to just look the other way. Not when he had your family to use as leverage to get David to do what he wanted."

"Not everyone is like your family, bear. All sane and normal. Some are vindictive and will agree to something only to make things worse in another way."

"What?" She turned to Styx. "How's his family different than others?"

"The Browns are close-knit. They live on an island outside of Nome. I doubt any of them would have left if Taber and Thorben hadn't mated with Kallie, and Thaddeus with Milo and Courtney. Kallie was kept prisoner for years and only began to come out of her shell since she came to the compound. She needs the security of where she is, and since the oldest Brown twins were already traveling back and forth between our land and the Brown Island, it made sense for them to stay with Kallie and travel to Nome occasionally. Thaddeus joined us because Milo is also an Elder guard for the clan."

"Wait, you mean they have more than one mate?"

"Twins Taber and Thorben were the first of my brothers to mate. They're the oldest and that's when the rest of us learned that our twins will have the same mate. My mother, Ava, explained that she had two fathers. Twins."

"But how?"

"Identical twins have the same DNA, which is why they normally end up with the same mate. It's rare for bear shifters to have twins, but my mother had two sets."

"Did the others mate together?"

Theodore nodded. "Not long ago they mated with Ivy. They've stayed on the island to help our father rule the sleuth. I'm the last of my siblings to mate, but it's worked down from the eldest and Mom believes mine will be soon."

"I don't understand. You said Milo was an Elder guard, is he a bear as well? If so, why is he guarding the Alaskan Tigers' Elders?"

"Tad—Thaddeus—is a bear, Milo is a tiger, and Courtney is human. They were destined to be together but we have no idea why when they're so different. Somehow they work," Styx answered. "I've never seen Milo as happy as he is now. His mates complete him."

"Frank said it was an abomination to have more than one mate." She wrapped her hands around the coffee mug that sat before her. "When I was eleven, I remember one of the tigresses of the clan had permission to visit a friend somewhere, and when she came back she was mated. Two tigers, I think. Frank had a fit."

"What did he do?" Styx pressed when she trailed off.

"I'm not sure. Those under the age of eighteen were sent back to our apartments. Back then I always thought they were just able to leave and carry on with their lives. Happily mated." She pushed the coffee away and glanced at Styx. "Now…"

"It's okay, Catnip, we don't need to relive these memories." He wiped a tear that had rolled down her cheek.

"He killed them." The words came out barely above a whisper, but it was like a weight was lifted from her chest. "Now I know that when the young children were ushered away, it's because a blood bath was about to erupt. If he had just killed them, everyone would have witnessed it. But he tortured them before he killed them. All because she was destined to be with more than one. She had no say in that, she didn't choose it, or plan to disobey him, and she still ended up dead."

"If David's the Alpha of the clan, it means Frank is dead and he can't hurt anyone else any longer."

"He did so much damage to everyone. Everyone was touched by his madness. What kind of long-term damage has that done to them? What mess will David have to clean up because of all the years under Frank's control?"

"Why don't we call him and find out?" Theodore suggested.

"One last question first. What about you? If all your brothers have mated with two, will you as well?"

"Only time will tell." Theodore brought the mug of coffee to his lips, but didn't take a sip. "I'll be happy either way. My only hope is that I can find someone I can bring home to the island. My woodshop is all set up there…no it's not even that because I can work anywhere but the island is my home. I might not do as much as Turi and Trey, but I don't want to leave them as the only ones running our family's sleuth."

"The bear just wants to find his mate."

"It's hard to know that you're next, and be stuck waiting." He set the mug aside. "Enough chatter about me. Let's make the call."

Unable to put it off any longer, she touched the mouse pad of the laptop in front of her. Ty had sent them the secure number where they could contact David once they made plans for their travel. Instead, she was contacting him before they even decided to go there. While the idea of seeing her brother on

107

the screen and knowing that he was okay excited her, it also terrified her. Dread chilled her veins at the possibility she'd find out something she didn't want to know. Something that would keep her from ever stepping foot on the clan's land again, and possibly from ever seeing her brother again.

"You're not going to find out the answers you need by just staring at the computer screen. You actually have to connect the call," Styx teased. "Come on, Catnip, whatever we find out, we'll deal with it. But we can't go to Connecticut blind."

"I know." She slid her finger up to the connect button. "Here goes nothing."

Styx rubbed his hand over her back. "Have faith."

Chapter Ten

It rang over and over until Mira was ready to hang up because she doubted David was around to answer it. Just as she slid the mouse to the disconnect button, his face filled the screen.

"David…" She couldn't keep the tears from sliding down her face. *He's alive.* Seeing him on the screen in front of her was the confirmation. She had never expected to see him again, or to enjoy the warmth of his smile. Only now there were lines around his eyes and no smile to be had. "I can't believe it…you're alive."

"You too, little sister. Where are you?"

"She's safe, that's what matters." Styx kept his hand on her back, rubbing small circle to ease the tension within her.

David's gaze slid over to him. "Who are you?"

"David." She drew her brother's attention back to her, not because she was ashamed of Styx, but because she didn't want him to have the same reaction as she did when she heard his name for the first time.

"Answer my question. Who are you with?"

"I was able to send a message to the Alaskan Tigers, and they sent me help. Theodore is from the Kodiak Bears." She tipped her head to the other side of her as he came around the counter and into view.

David barely looked at Theodore. "Who's the one next to you?"

"Styx—"

"Get away from my sister!" David hollered. Fear and anger had his eyes shifting to the warm orange fire of his tiger. "She did nothing. Frank is dead. I'm the new Alpha of this clan and—"

"Stop this." She raised her voice. "Just listen to me for a minute before you start screaming at him."

"Don't be naïve, Mira. You must have *seen* that he's dangerous." There was no doubt he meant through her visions.

"Dangerous, no doubt." Styx snarled. "But not to her. I would never hurt my—"

"Stop." She cut him off before he could say mate. That was the last thing she needed at the moment. "David, he came to my rescue and saved me from some assholes in D.C. He's not here to hurt me, and he didn't come after me on Frank's orders. He came because Ty and Tabitha sent him."

"He's there to kill you. Can you get away from him? Or tell me where you are, and I'll send someone to help you."

"If you could just be quiet for a moment, I'll explain," she snapped as her own annoyance began to seep through. "As you've put it, I've *seen* things, and Styx isn't here to kill me."

"How do you know that? Have you had another vision?" David cut her off again.

"Tell him the whole thing," Styx whispered.

"She can speak for herself. Don't encourage her to lie for you."

Out of view of the screen, she placed her hand on Styx's leg and tried to soak up his comfort. When she made this call, all she could think about was the outcome of what happened to her family and clan. She hadn't considered his reaction to Styx. Maybe that was because she had already accepted him. "He's my mate." She just wanted to move past this so they could get to the reason she'd called.

"What?" David rose from the chair he was sitting in. "Tell me you didn't!"

"The mating is complete," Styx answered. "Now do you believe I mean her no harm?"

"She'll be in more danger than she was under Frank's rule."

"No." Styx wrapped his arm around her shoulders and pulled her close. "She'll be protected. I will keep her safe, because people know what I'm capable of."

"Stop it, both of you. Now, this isn't the reason I called. Tell me what happened after I left."

"I don't like this, Mira." David glanced between her and Styx for a moment before finally shaking his head. "Shelly was killed and all hell broke loose."

"Shel." The grief she'd been holding back since she'd run from Connecticut rushed forward. She couldn't hold onto a ray of hope that things hadn't gone as bad as she feared, and that everyone was still alive.

"She got what was coming to her." David's tone was harsh, but his eyes held a hint of sadness. "She had been pressing the boundaries with Frank for months, and the little punishments he handed down to her were no longer working. Even my agreement with him wasn't stopping him any longer. I warned her there would be nothing I could do for her if she continued to disobey him, but she didn't listen. That night she realized how much trouble she was in. The simple act of sneaking out had been the final straw, and Frank was going to be sure she paid for everything she had done the last few months. It's why she betrayed your trust."

"Was anyone else killed besides her and Frank?"

David nodded. "A number of clan members including Mom. She tried to save Shelly, and Frank killed her. That's when things really started to get out of hand. Dad is taking it hard, blames himself since he wasn't there when things happened. He was out on some errand for Frank."

"Both Shelly and Mom…all because of me."

"No." David sat back down. "Shelly made her own choice, and the consequences most likely would have been the same. Frank had grown tired of her disobedience. You saw what he did to her last time. She barely survived the whipping, but she didn't learn. Mom always tried to protect Shelly because she was the youngest, and she knew what could happen if she got in the way when Frank was like that."

"How did you survive?" Styx questioned.

"I had been in what you might consider a leadership role over the land for nearly a year now. Many were used to having orders handed down from me. After…" He glanced at her as if he realized whatever he was about to say needed to be rephrased. He finally settled on the word he wanted to use. "Everything. I stepped up to regain control and I've taken over the clan. It's small now, and needed someone to step into command."

"Small? We were small before, but the way you say that makes me believe it's worse."

"Fifteen." David squeezed the bridge of his nose and let out a deep sigh. "That includes Dad and I. It's why I had hoped you'd return home, but I see that's not an option now. I don't believe visiting would be wise." He glanced at Styx.

"But Dad…"

"I'll see to him. Give it a little time, and we can make arrangements either for him to meet you somewhere safe, or for you to come here for a visit. Right now, things are too uncertain. I can't guarantee your safety, not as long as *he's* by your side, and I have no doubt he won't let you come alone."

"That would be correct. She's my mate and I won't send her there alone," Styx agreed. "I appreciate you thinking of your sister's safety."

"If you were concerned with her safety, you'd have never mated with her."

"David." She let out a huff, and wanted to tell him that Styx wasn't the man Frank had made them believe. In the end, she kept her mouth shut because Styx was right about one thing: his reputation kept people safe. Now that she was on the other side of things, she could see the benefit in it.

"We understand your decision," Styx said. "You might want to consider meeting her somewhere in the near future with your father." He steered the conversation back on track.

David glared at him for a moment before finally nodding. "I'll speak with our father in the coming days, and we can see about arrangements for them."

"I meant for you, too. All of you have suffered great loss, but for Mira it's worse. She's lost the clan she was raised in, one she might never even be able to visit again. The reassurance of seeing both of you would be good for not only her, but all of you."

"He's right. I'd really like to see you, David." She wiped tears from her cheeks.

"I can't get away from the clan now, but when I can we'll work something out."

"There's one more thing before you go. Are you a supporter, or are you against us?" Styx asked without missing a beat.

"I told Ty I would give him an answer as soon as I could."

"I know what you told my Alpha, but from what Mira told me of that night, and how you don't seem to be angry at her for her position, I believe you already knew her stance," Styx pushed. "Did Shelly tell you, or did you know because you were a supporter as well?"

"My stance is my own business."

"Not if you're against what Tabitha's trying to do," Mira said. She tried to swallow the lump in her throat, but it was an unmovable object. If he was against Tabitha, against everything she believed in, he'd be an enemy and she knew what happened to those who stood against them.

"Right now, I have to think of what's good for the clan." David sidestepped the question again. "My personal beliefs are mine and mine alone. With the clan numbers so small, I can't afford to lose anyone else. We're already small enough as it is, and we could be prey to the larger clans who wish to expand."

"If you're a supporter, we can provide you with additional support," Styx said. "No one will try to take over your clan. If you're willing to take in others, we can make your land a safe haven for those escaping Alphas like Frank. We need places people can go if they are forced to run like Mira was."

"That night, you weren't surprised." She adjusted on the bar stood. "You knew. But how? Shelly didn't tell you, or she'd have betrayed you as well and told Frank that you knew but never told him. No one else knew. So how did you?"

David leaned back in his chair, a smirk clear across his face. "There were things you said that couldn't have been taken any other way."

"You…" She was unable to finish her thought.

"Yes. I've been watching as things happened in the shifter world, and as Tabitha began to take her place. What she wants to do is something I completely support. However, as an Alpha now, I need to consider my clan. That means I must decide if committing to Tabitha's cause publically is the best thing for us. None of the members here have any kind of training. As an Alpha, I'm totally vulnerable without guards."

"We can help with that. We can send a couple to help protect you, and train those you select," Styx offered.

"I appreciate it, and I'll weigh that with my decision." David nodded. "I need some time to consider everything, but I'll be in touch soon." David stared at Styx for a moment before adding, "I don't care what your reputation is, or the fact I couldn't win in a fair fight against you even if I tried, but know this. If you hurt my sister in any way, I'll make you pay. Your life will be hell, and you'll wish you were dead long before it happened."

"David," she scolded.

"It's okay," Styx interrupted. "He's only showing his concern, and he has nothing to worry about." He looked back at the screen. "You have my word she'll be safe, and if you know much about me, you know that I never break my word."

"Dad and I will be in touch soon, Mira. Until then, stay safe." With that, David leaned forward and clicked to end the call.

She couldn't pull her gaze from the computer screen, even as the call screen went dark. Only fifteen members of her clan had survived. It had to have been a bloodbath after she left. So much death. How many more would die because of the decisions of that night? Would David be in danger now? Would he be in more danger or less if he committed to Tabitha?

"Catnip…" Styx called to her. "Are you okay?"

"Is she in shock?" Theodore came to her other side to look at her.

"I'm fine, just thinking. So much has changed."

"Not all for the bad, Catnip." He pulled her tighter against him. "It brought you to me. Your clan is now free of Frank."

"But David is in danger."

"We'll do what we can for him, but unless he supports Tabitha, there's no way we can send guards to help him."

"If he's a supporter, I'll go to Connecticut and help train the clan," Theodore offered.

"Thank you." She smiled up at him. "I appreciate it. I just wish I could have gone there to see them."

"It might have been for the best that we wait." Theodore pulled out the last bar stool and sat down. "Right now, even though the clan is small, there's a battle going on within it. They need to work out their issues before outsiders can come in. While you might have been a member, you're not anymore. David needs time to establish his rule as Alpha, and until then he can't protect anyone outside of the clan."

"I know you're right, but I just lost half my family and I feel like my place is there with Dad and David." She glanced at Styx. "But I want to be here with you. My tigress claws my insides at the very thought of being away from you."

"We'll be together. Not here, but in Alaska, and soon we'll see your family. Right now, Theodore is right. David needs time to get the clan under his control."

She let her head rest against his shoulder. She knew she should be happy that David and her father were alive, but grief poured through every cell in her body. The loss of her mother was more painful than that of Shelly. *Shel, you were my best friend, but I warned you Frank would only let you push so much before he'd strike back...*

They had managed to push off their departure from the West Virginia Tigers' land by an additional day, giving Mira and Styx more time to enjoy each other before they had to get back to the Alaskan Tigers and his duties. He was thankful for the extra time with her, even if they were stuck in a cabin with Theodore, because it gave him time to get to know her. There was so much more to her. More he wanted to explore. He felt as though he had barely touched the surface on discovering his mate.

Theodore, Mira, Summer, Jinx, Lukas, and Styx sat gathered around the table in the Elders' house. They had just finished lunch and were waiting while another table that had been a family heirloom was loaded onto the plane for

Theodore to restore to the beautiful piece it had once been.

Everything was returning to a semblance of normalcy, or at least as normal as their world could get. Things had calmed down in Washington D.C., and the tigers there had yet to cause an issue. Though he suspected that one day, not far in the future, they'd seek retaliation for the clan members Styx and Theodore had killed.

Quinn was still pissed they'd been in his territory without alerting him. The black panther was on his own, without a clan's backing, but for some reason he thought his status as United States Marshal gave him a higher pecking order. It might be that way with humans, but it held little weight when it came to the shifter world.

Now they could only sit back and wait to see what happened as David tried to take over the Connecticut Tigers. Styx and the others would be there if he chose to commit to Tabitha and the future of their species, and they'd help in any way they could. If he chose not to, there was nothing any of them could do. He glanced over at his mate, and for her sake he hoped that things would work out for David's claim to Alpha. She had already lost her sister and mother. She didn't need to lose anyone else.

He pushed his thoughts away and leaned forward, his gaze moving toward Lukas, who sat at the opposite end of the table from Jinx. "How do you like your new role?"

"It took a bit of getting used to, but I was born for this. Eric has learned quickly what I expect from him as far as the Nerd Crew goes, and has been a great help to both myself and Connor. Now I'm able to focus on my duties as the Lieutenant of the clan."

"He's been exceptional, and having him has given me more time to spend with Summer and Claire," Jinx added.

"How's Claire doing?"

"She's beginning to open up and talk a little," Summer answered. "She has really taken to Jackson. I think it's something about his voice because she loves to bring him a book and curl up in his lap as he reads it to her. She's growing comfortable with Carson and Meshell as well."

"Meshell? You have a female guard?" Mira's tone held a note of shock.

Summer nodded. "Surprised?"

"I didn't think many clans allowed female guards."

"It goes against everything in some Alphas but times are changing. If a woman is capable of the job, they should be allowed to do it," Jinx answered. "It might be old-fashioned, but women are precious and should be protected. Not put in the front lines but Meshell has proved herself, and she's an excellent guard for Claire. We've discussed this extensively, and it's likely that Meshell will be appointed as the Captain of Claire's Guards. We have yet to appoint someone because we've been waiting for her to get comfortable around everyone and settle into the clan. Jackson is Summer's Captain of the Guards, so that eliminates him. Since there's more possible danger to Summer, I'm unwilling to reassign him."

"They're not the only ones with a female guard. Shadow is the Captain of Bethany's Guards, with me as her second. She's ruthless and started at an early age to make a name for herself," Styx reminded her.

A throat cleared behind them, and everyone turned to find Red standing there. "The table has been loaded and the plane is fueled."

"Thank you." Theodore rose from his seat. "I'll go get the plane ready, go over the pre-flight checklist, and I'll see you down there."

"We'll be along in a few minutes," Styx told him.

"Jinx and Summer, thank you for everything. It was a pleasure to see you again."

"You, too, Theodore. Be sure to come back. Claire is anxious to play with *her teddy* again." Summer gave him a warm smile.

He shook his head and headed out of the room. Silence had fallen over them, but Styx was tugged toward the memories of Theodore in his bear form playing with Claire. It was almost as if they had stumbled upon a private moment.

"Mira…" Summer started, and paused until she looked at her. "If you ever need anything or someone to talk to, I'm here. I have an idea what you're going through because I had to leave my clan when they were in the middle of a change. My brother, Ben, is the Lieutenant to the Texas Tigers. It's hard to leave your home, your family, and everything you've known to start over with a mate you've only just met, but it's worth it."

"I heard about the Texas Tigers, and how Avery went on a killing spree before he was finally taken down. Most of his clan was killed."

Styx placed his hand over hers. "You'll have to forgive her," he said. "Frank brainwashed his clan about a lot of things. He told them of the Texas Tigers in order to strike fear in the members. He said Ty and Tabitha were ordering anyone who stood against them to be eliminated. While I told her that Tex was a former member of the clan before he took over in Texas, we haven't had time to go through all of what Frank told them versus reality."

"There's nothing to apologize for. Avery was very much the same. Anything he thought he could use to gain more control, he used it." Summer leaned forward and took Jinx's hand. "It wasn't until I mated with Jinx and came here that I understood how a clan was supposed to be."

"It's disgusting that Alphas do this." Mira shook her head.

"You have to deal with crazy people in all walks of life. Shifters are no different," Jinx agreed. "However, Tabitha is the key to changing all of that."

"Hopefully, the future looks brighter than the past I just came from." She glanced at Styx.

"It will be, Catnip, it will be." Styx squeezed her hand as a ray of hope sparked within him. Each of them had accepted things, and they were moving past it. Their future was together.

Chapter Eleven

Thousands of feet in the air, Styx sat in his seat with his stomach churning. He needed something to keep his mind occupied. He teased his thumb over the arches of Mira's knuckles and tried to focus on the peaks and valleys on them. The tiger within wanted to explore other parts of her.

He'd only had a few days with her, but in a few hours he'd be back to his duties to Bethany and the Alaskan Tigers. He'd have to find a balance when all he wanted to do was ravish his mate. Even though not going to Connecticut was the safest option, he couldn't help be a little disappointed by the fact he didn't have more time with her before he had to get back to his commitments. Maybe in a few days, as long as things were still going smoothly, he could convince Ty that he deserved a break with his mate and slip off to one of the cabins the Brown family owned. Seclusion was just what the two of them needed in order to get to know each other better.

"Do you think David is going to be okay?" She continued to stare out the window.

"If he can act like a leader and bring them all together, then yes, I believe he's got a good chance. The clan needs a strong Alpha to unite them and help them move past what has happened. Everyone there would have lost someone, and that will form a bond. He killed Frank, and he needs to show them that he didn't do it just because Shelly was killed, but to avenge all of those who died that day and to free them. He's given them a chance to leave, and no one else has. That alone shows that they support him."

"But the clan is so small."

"He's going to have outside threats, especially if it's public knowledge that Frank kept the members weak and unable to fight back." He squeezed her hand. "I've offered him a chance to help himself and the clan. All he has to do is commit to Tabitha. I promise you that if he's on our side we'll help him in whatever ways we can. As an Alpha, he'll need to stand on his own feet and keep control, but we can provide temporary guards to keep him and the clan safe. Training the members, so they'll be able to protect themselves and their land. You know our species won't stand for someone else always stepping in to save the day, so he'll have to make the Connecticut Tigers strong. Small numbers don't always mean prey."

"Not always, but they are."

"He's got challenges ahead of him, but if he gives it his all, he can overcome them." He didn't know what else to say to help ease her fears. "Have you seen anything in your visions?"

"No." She turned to him. "Nothing. Not even a glimmer, but maybe I'm trying too hard. It's not like my visions come at will, they just happen, and not regularly either. I knew you'd find me, but I knew nothing about what Shelly would do that night. It's like the visions pick and choose what they tell me."

"It's going to be okay. It's possible your visions will come if you don't try to force them." He rubbed her hand and she turned back to the window. There was nothing he could say that would make this easier. Only time would help. Time and if David committed to Tabitha so they could send support his way. It might take months before it was safe enough for her to visit her old clan again, but just the knowledge that they were safe, and being led by her brother, would give her peace of mind.

The tension from her traveled through their bond, making him more on edge. The turbulence that had returned wasn't helping matters, but he sat there silently, his thumb traveling over her knuckles. Over and over again in small circles, one knuckle at a time, while he focused on the journey from one to another.

"That doesn't seem to be working." She nodded to his thumb exploration. "How about we find another way?"

"What did you have in mind?" His teeth were gritted as the plane was tossed around in turbulence.

"Something that involves us both getting naked." She wiggled her eyebrows at him. "I've always wanted to have sex on a plane, and now seems to be a very good time."

"You're insane."

"Why? Can't my big old tiger get it up?" She tugged her sweater over her head. "Or maybe I just don't turn you on."

"A challenge I shall rise to. Catnip, you're truly beautiful."

"Then come on." She stood and kicked off her shoes. "It will be easier to do it with me braced against the edge of the table."

"Well, I guess, unlike in a vehicle, if we crash seatbelts will do very little to save us." He unhooked his seatbelt and followed after her, careful to avoid the trail of clothes she left in her wake.

She leaned against the table. "Theodore will keep us safely in the skies and within minutes, you'll forget we're flying." She took hold of his shirt and slid it up his chest. "Mmm. There's something sexy about you when you're trying to hide your terror. The way your muscles tighten and show off all their beauty." She slid her hands over his chest.

The sensation of these intimate touches were something he'd never thought he'd experience. Now he hoped he'd never get accustomed to them, that they'd always be new and fresh like they were at that moment, sparking excitement through every cell of his body.

His hands slid over her naked body as she leaned against the table and desire rose within him. He wanted her unlike anything he'd ever experienced. Forgetting they were bouncing around the sky, he pressed his lips to hers. The sweetness of her vanilla lip-gloss and the spice of her tigress urged him on. Slipping his tongue between her lips, he devoured her. His beast rose to the surface, mingling with hers as the heat rose between them. He kissed along her jawline until he reached the sweet spot just below her ear. Grazing his teeth over the area, he blew his cool breath against her flushed skin. "I think this was the best idea you've ever had."

"Mile high club, here we come."

"Is it really the same if you're on a private plane?" He nuzzled against the nape of her neck.

"Yes, because we could never do this on a public charter. All your growling would scare the passengers, not to mention your roar when you finish. You're pretty full of yourself, mate, but I guess that's only to be expected with your skills."

"I guess we'll have to take what we can get." He slid his hands from around her back to cup her breasts. The smooth skin as it arched from her body had his shaft straining against the roughness of his jeans. His thumb slid over the bud of her nipple and it hardened under his touch.

He dipped his head and claimed her nipple with his teeth, then gently tugged, making it hard before moving over to the next one. Without breaking contact, he lifted her up to sit on the edge of the table. She wiggled against him and a soft moan escaped her.

"Your moans would make it undeniable what we were doing as well," he teased.

With a soft moan, she pulled him closer. "I've always wanted to make love on an airplane, so you can't blame a girl for getting in the mood. Now, off with these jeans."

"Oh, Catnip. I don't think there's a better distraction than this. We might have to fly more often." He unzipped his jeans, letting them fall down his legs. He didn't have the will power to stop to take off his boots and pants completely. He needed her now.

She stared at him while sliding her hand down his chest until she found his shaft. Her fingers wrapped around it, and she rubbed down the length, painstakingly slow.

"Stop that, or I'm not going to last." It came out more of a growl than he had expected.

"We can't have that." She slid her hand down the length of him, until her fingers circled around the tip of his shaft. "It would spoil the fantasy, and we'd have to do it again."

"We have several hours of flight left, but I'll keep Theodore flying for as long as we need." The words were bit off as she squeezed tighter, working back up his manhood. He needed her. "As good as this feels, and damn it does, I want to be inside of you. My tiger wants to join us together until you're screaming my name as ecstasy engulfs you."

"Take me." She let her hand fall away from his shaft, placing her hands on either side of her as she leaned back.

He took hold of her hips and slid her to the very edge of the table. He adjusted so his shaft teased over the folds before pushing his way inside. As he entered her, a moan tore from her lips and she pushed against him, speeding his entry. He held tight to her hips, working his way into the tight passage at his own pace.

As his shaft finally slid home, she reached up and took hold of his shoulders. "Don't make me wait. I need you hard and fast."

"As you wish." He gripped her hips and began working in and out of her.

Each time, harder and faster. Slamming his length into her, joining them in a way only mates were joined. Their bodies rocked back and forth, each thrust gaining momentum. The plane's gentle sway added a new sensation as their ecstasy grew within them.

She grabbed his hips and arched toward him. With every thrust, she pushed against him. Her tiny budding nipples stood to attention, screaming for him to suck on them. Without losing his rhythm, he dipped his head and drew his tongue along each nipple, blowing gently on them.

"Styx," she cried, her release within reach as she dug her nails into the skin of his hips.

Wanting to watch her face as she came around him, he leaned back, taking hold of her hips and speeding his pace. Tension had her muscles constricting around him as her orgasm neared, bringing his own ecstasy closer. Her face came to life with a glow as the world exploded around them, as if they were the only two people in existence.

He claimed her lips, wanting their bodies to be joined in every way as he filled her with his seed. Against his lips, she screamed his name, and it was all he needed to send him over the edge. His balls tightened, and he growled as he climaxed. Abruptly, he ended the kiss, tipped his head back, and let out the roar that had been building within him.

He stayed buried within her as their breathing returned to normal. The warm burn of fresh claw marks tingled along the curve of his hips, but he didn't care. His mate had marked him, and he was honored to wear her stripes.

"Sorry." She ran a finger just below the marks on one side.

"Don't be. You can mark me anytime." He wrapped his arms around her, and snuggled her against his body. "My beautiful Catnip, I'm falling in love with you." He rubbed his face into the crook of her shoulder, marking her as his.

The intercom crackled to life. "Next time, a warning would be nice. One minute all is fine, and the next all I hear are growls and roars. A bear could think you two were fighting."

"Jealous," Styx teased as he slid free from Mira. "Here's your warning: it might happen again."

"Might?" She teased the tip of her finger along his chest. "I'm counting on it."

Preview: Healing the Clan

Alaskan Tigers Book Ten

David is left to pick up the pieces of the Connecticut Tigers and protect what remains of the clan as their many enemies descend upon them. Now that he is Alpha, most of the clan is looking to him for answers. At the same time, others want him to seek revenge on the one they blame for the fall of their clan and the death of their loved ones. He must find a balance between justice and protecting what is left of his family.

Victoria escaped the Connecticut Tigers clan years ago to seek out her own path, or at least that's what she wanted everyone to believe. In truth, she couldn't deal with the former Alpha's demands any longer. Now that he's dead, she must make the journey home. It is time for the truth to come to light and for those who survived to live again.

The clan has been suppressed for so long, its members have forgotten how to live without someone controlling every aspect of their lives. The clan will face many challenges ahead, but those may not be the ones they expected.

Chapter One

For weeks, David had been trying to piece together his badly damaged clan. With only fifteen members remaining, it was appalling the level of destruction they had suffered at the hands of the former Alpha. He should have challenged Frank years before and taken over the Connecticut Tigers, but it was tragedy that finally forced him to make his move. When his youngest sister, Shelly, made a stupid decision, it had not only resulted in her death and the deaths of many members of the clan, but it almost killed his other sister, Mira, as well. The clan was ravaged by disaster, and every time he attempted to put it back together, something else would fall apart.

If things inside the clan weren't bad enough, shifters were sniffing at his territory. Alphas wanted to expand their rule, and Lieutenants sought to strike out on their own and overtake the Connecticut Tigers. They were beginning to close in on him, and soon he'd have to battle to keep his clan—a battle he wasn't sure he'd win, especially if multiple parties descended on them at once.

His combat skills were minimal at best. Since taking over the clan, he had been working hard to ready himself but the clan's needs came first. Now, he regretted that decision. As the threats intensified, he was almost helpless to defend himself and the clan. Under Frank's control, none of them had been trained as guards. At this point, it was now or never.

He had always planned on committing to the Queen of the Tigers, Tabitha, and the future she was trying to build for the shifter population, once he got the clan under his rule. They had been through so much that adding another adjustment they had to overcome would make things harder. With their current volatile situation, he questioned his decision to wait.

His sister Mira's last comment to him ran through his thoughts: *A safe world for our kind without Alphas like Frank—what could be so bad about that?*

"Nothing."

"What was that?" Tim, his father, strolled across the living area. Even in his mid-sixties, his father remained toned with only a few gray hairs mixed into the light brown, adding character instead of age.

"I was just thinking about Mira and the offer again." He met his father's gaze and waited for his disapproval to show. One of the biggest disagreements they had since he took over was committing to Tabitha. His father wanted nothing to do with that and couldn't see any of the benefits or changes she'd bring to their population.

"It's your choice. You are, after all, the Alpha here. Who am I to question your judgment?"

"Dad, that's exactly what I'm trying to stop."

"An Alpha's role is to be the dictator over the clan." Tim sank down into the chair across from David as if a ton of bricks rested on his shoulders. "You need to remember that. Otherwise they're going to kill you. I've lost enough already. I don't want to add my son's death to that list."

Family dynamics might be different for tigers than for humans, but his family had lived in one room his whole life. This resulted in them building a weird relationship. He wouldn't say they were close but definitely closer than a lot of shifter families. Lately, a new tension had developed between him and his father he wasn't sure how to deal with. Dad hadn't just lost his youngest daughter, but his mate had also been killed at Frank's hands. Still, David suspected his father blamed him and Mira for the loss. They might not have been the ones who took their lives, but it was Mira's support of Tabitha that had turned the bad situation into a disastrous one. While she was safe in Alaska with her new mate, David was stuck here trying to deal with the outcome.

He had been keeping Dad's attitude from Mira so she wouldn't worry additionally about them. He wouldn't allow her to come to Connecticut yet, and he hadn't been able to leave the clan to see her, so all they had were a few short video messages every few days. Things were too unsafe for her there at the moment, and having her mate by her side would only make things worse with the clan. Frank had instilled fear in the members, vowing to hand them over to Styx if they didn't obey. Torture and death proved more than enough of a deterrent to convince them to fall into line. No one had known Styx was no longer the bogeyman of the tiger world. He had given up the life of an assassin to join Tabitha and the Alaskan Tigers as an Elders guard.

Even knowing things had changed with him didn't eliminate all of David's concerns that his sister was mated to a former assassin. While she might be protected from some of his enemies, there would be others who would see her as a way to take revenge on Styx. He didn't like the new danger that now surrounded her.

"Are you even listening to me?" Dad's voice cut through his thoughts.

"Yes, Dad." He nearly growled before he regained control of his frustration. "I'm ruling this clan the best I can."

"Siding with them isn't going to make things easier."

"I know you're against it, but it's for the best. You need to accept this is what's needed at this time. This clan won't survive without some help. Mira's right—"

"I don't want to hear about Mira."

"Dad." He took a deep breath. Mira was a sensitive subject between them because, as far as their father was concerned, she had been the root of what happened and had betrayed their family. Although not the truth, it was what he felt, so there was no use trying to change it. "You might not want to hear it, but she's right. There are worse things for our kind than what Tabitha and Ty are trying to do. Alphas who like how Frank used to operate need to be eliminated."

"Frank was a good man, and if you'd run this clan like he did, you'd be a great Alpha."

"Enough!" He jumped to his feet and began to pace. "This is my clan, and because you are my father, I've listened to your comments—but no longer. I'm not Frank and never will be him. I won't run this clan as he did. He was a vindictive Alpha who brainwashed and tortured his members."

Tim glared at him, anger seeping off him. "I thought pushing you toward him and having you as his right hand man would have taught you something."

"It did teach me something. It taught me how *not* to do things. Being an Alpha is more than ordering people around. An Alpha is responsible for his people's safety and well-being."

"Enough. You'll do what you want, so let's just leave it at that."

A knock on the door interrupted David's response. "What is it?"

The door opened, and Ryder stepped through. "Sir." He bowed as Frank had always required but it only served to upset David.

"You don't need to do that," David reminded him. It didn't matter how many times he told the clan they didn't need to bow whenever they came before him. Years of conditioning under Frank wouldn't be erased overnight.

"I'm sorry to interrupt, sir."

"Don't worry, Ryder. I'm leaving." Tim stood and walked toward the door. "You and our *Alpha* can deal with whatever brought you here."

Even as his father left the room, anger rose in him. While in private, Dad had made little effort to hide the fact he believed David wasn't running the clan as he should. His tone as he uttered *Alpha* marked the first time he'd revealed his disgust to another. If Ryder caught the snide comment, he didn't acknowledge it.

"Come in, Ryder, and tell me whatever new issue has arisen."

Ryder stepped farther into the room. "Some of the clan members are in an uproar because Heidi is packing. They see her brother arriving this evening to take her away as another loss to our family."

"Is this what she wants, or what her family is demanding?" Heidi had come from another clan when she mated one of their members. He was trying to remember the details but all he could think at the moment was it was somewhere out west and that her family had been unhappy when she had come there.

"I tried to speak with her, but she's extremely upset and it's difficult to understand what she wants. She says one thing and then another. It's unfortunate because we've lost so much already. I was hoping you might be able to talk to her. If this is her decision, then I'll make sure the clan members understand and support her instead of making it harder on her. She's already suffered a great deal. We all have."

David watched the man before him and appreciated the eye contact. Ryder was unlike the other members of the clan who barely looked at him and would have never come to his quarters, a thought that made David once again consider promoting him to Lieutenant. He'd had the initiative to speak with Heidi and try to calm the clan members before seeking out the Alpha, which granted him another point in David's book.

"Bring her here. I'll speak with her."

"Yes, sir." He started to bow before he stopped himself with a shy smile. "Sorry, old habits die hard…"

"Once this is settled, we need to have a discussion as well." Something clicked in that moment, and he made the decision to promote him. This was his first decision as an Alpha and for the clan, but it wouldn't be the last.

While he waited for Ryder to return with Heidi, he glanced around the Alpha quarters. He had effected minimal changes but there were other things he wanted to do. His list was growing, but once he had a Lieutenant he could count on, there would hopefully be less to stress about. The clan was important to him and, if they were going to survive, he had to make their safety a priority. If there was one thing Frank had taught him, it was that a clan had to be run with an iron fist. Anything less would leave him open to challenges. He wouldn't be vindictive or torture his members, but there would be no doubt as to who held control. Their sustained future and survival demanded that much from him.

He grabbed his phone from the makeshift desk he had constructed near the window so he could look out over the clan's grounds as he worked. Green grass stretched ahead for as far as the eye could see. The summer would be coming to a close soon, and the cool winds of fall would blow colorful leaves all over their land. As he looked out, he realized there was one thing missing. *Homes*—it was something he wanted to rectify, and soon. With only fifteen members, fourteen if Heidi left, they deserved their own space.

All his life, his family of five—his parents, two sisters, and he—had lived in one room. He wanted better for the clan and he'd make that happen. They were moving into the future, and that meant they needed to stand on their own feet. They must get out and spread their wings. No longer would they live in rooms that were nearly as dark as tunnels with one small window per unit that wasn't even big enough for someone to climb out of because Frank was always concerned with people trying to leave after curfew.

"Frank, you sure did a number on us. It will be years before we function like other clans. I'm going to fix this." He slid his finger over the cell phone screen and unlocked it. The time had come for him to vow his commitment to Tabitha, the Alaskan Tigers, and the future of their population. This decision would cost him, and he only hoped he was doing the right thing.

He shot a quick text to Mira. *I'm ready. Set things up with the Elders.*

Being mated to Styx, one of the Elder guards of the Alaskan Tigers, she'd have a better chance of setting up a conference call without him having to interfere with their schedules. Having her deal with that would also allow him to handle Heidi's situation first.

With the text sent, he slid his phone into the pocket of his jeans and glanced down at the pad on the table. His to-do list stared up at him without a single thing crossed off. It seemed like it was getting longer by the minute.

Ryder stood in the doorway. "Sir, if you're ready."

"Bring her in." He moved away from the desk and back to the sitting area with the hope that it would seem less formal and intimidating.

"Heidi, he's ready to see you now."

The young woman with golden brown hair that fell around her shoulders stepped into the room. Terror filled her eyes as she looked toward him. The loss of her mate had left dark circles under her eyes, and no longer was there a smile on her face or a sparkle in her eyes. The Heidi who had come to the clan a few months ago was no longer standing before him. Only the shell of the woman remained. Losing a mate was like losing part of yourself. Mating brought two pieces together and made both of them whole. Now that he was gone, Heidi would need time to grieve and adjust, but she would always know that he had died protecting her.

"Sir..." Her voice cracked as she bowed to show her respect.

"Come have a seat, Heidi." He didn't bother to tell her the bow wasn't necessary as he gestured toward the sofa.

Out of the remaining clan members, she was the only one who hadn't vowed her loyalties to him. When the rest of the clan had done it, she had been distraught over her mate and he had another member escort her to her private quarters. As the weeks passed, he hadn't pressed, giving her time to grieve and decide what she wanted. Even now, he wouldn't force it, except the current situation required that she make a decision to stay or return home. If she wanted to stay, he couldn't fight her family and her former clan without her commitment to him as her Alpha.

"I'll wait in the hall in case you need me." Ryder turned back to the door.

"Join us."

There was a moment of shock and maybe a dash of fear before Ryder joined them in the sitting area.

With Heidi on one end of the sofa and Ryder on the other, David took the chair. "Ryder informed me of your leaving."

"With Brad gone…" She took a deep breath and visibly tried to force the tears away. "I don't belong here any longer."

"This is your choice?" He made sure it was a question instead of a statement, but she didn't answer. "You don't have to leave. This is your home if you wish to stay."

"It's been made clear that it isn't." Tears rolled down her cheeks. "My brother will be arriving soon, and he'll escort me…"

"You paused just than because you couldn't say *home*. That might be where your family is, but it's not home to you anymore, is it?" When she didn't answer, he continued. "I'm telling you that you can stay here. No one else's opinion matters unless they plan to challenge me for my position of Alpha."

"My family has made it clear I'm not safe here."

He scooted his chair closer to her. "Things will be changing, and soon those who threaten us won't be an issue any longer. I'll make sure you're safe if you want to stay."

"Walter's made it clear…" She shook her head and covered her mouth with her hand.

"Sir, if I may," Ryder interrupted. When David nodded, he continued. "Brad's father, Walter, was so upset over his son's death that he's said some nasty comments about Heidi."

"Upset over Brad's death!" Heidi raged. "I'm his mate, but Walter made it sound as though he was the only one who mattered. Even now, Brad's…remains are with him. He won't let me have that last piece of my mate." Sadness, fury, and undeniable grief coated her outrage.

"I'll deal with Walter and see that Brad's remains are returned to you." He laid a hand over hers. "If you want to stay here, you're welcome. I'll make sure you have no additional problems with him."

"They don't want me here," she mumbled through her tears.

"I'm Alpha here, not them," he gently reminded her. "Losing Brad was a great loss to our clan and to me personally. I considered him a good friend, as I do you, and I would hate to see you leave here because of Walter. You know he was a big supporter of Frank, and losing them both has cut deep for him. Instead of cherishing the last connection he has to Brad, he's pushing you away because of his own grief."

"I'm grieving, too, but I'm not acting like that." Her words came out as more of a whine than anything else.

"I know, but you've always been a stronger person than him. You've come to a new clan to make a home with your mate. You dealt with Walter's hatred, Frank's vindictive attitude, and some of the clan's displeasure at having an outsider come into our land when many were unmated within our ranks. Yet, somehow, in the months you've been here, you've made this your home. You became a part of the community. You have friends here, and while I know they can't replace the loss of your mate, they can stand beside you while you grieve and help you through it." He squeezed her hand. "Heidi, you've seen the clan at its worst, and now that I'm in control, things are going to change. I'm going to make it better. Stay."

"My brother wants me to come home."

"What do you want?" Ryder pressed. "You're not committed to any Alpha at the moment, so you get to make this decision without that pressure. Do you want to go back to your old Alpha or stay here under David? You know David's not going to run the clan like Frank did. He and Brad were good friends. He'll make sure you're safe and happy here."

"Ryder's right, but this needs to be your decision. If you want to stay, you'll have to vow your loyalty to me. Only then can I fight to keep you here. I'll make the call to your brother and former Alpha, so you won't have to worry about explaining things to them. No matter your decision, I'm going to deal with Walter."

They sat there in silence for several minutes. David didn't want to pressure her, but he wasn't sure how long he could stand the silence before he said something. He would do whatever she wanted, and if that meant her leaving, he'd support her decision. Brad was a close friend, or at least as close as they could become despite David's previous position under Frank. Because of that, he wanted to make sure Heidi was happy. The silence was approaching the uncomfortable stage when she finally nodded.

"I want to stay. My memories of him are here, and I want to see the clan move beyond Frank and into the light. It's what Brad would have wanted. He tried so hard to protect the members of this clan. He died to protect me. The best way to honor his memory is to stay here and do my part."

"Then we will make it so." David nodded. "You're giving up an opportunity to return home to your family and a stable clan. I will do my best to ensure you don't regret it."

"Thank you." She wiped her tears away, leaving behind wet streaks on her cheeks. "I know you'll do whatever is best for the clan, and that's what matters. I'll help in any way I can."

"I'm glad you said that." He released her hand and leaned back in his chair. "The coming days and weeks are going to be a big adjustment, and I want your help. We're a small clan, but most of us don't interact with each other much. Frank forbade socializing, so the only times we were all together were for unfortunate occasions and our meals. That needs to change. We will no longer be prisoners."

"What do you want me to do?"

"The clan is going to need support, especially the widowed mates. I want you to help them to adjust, console each other, and assist them accept what I will be announcing soon." He glanced back at Ryder. "I'm telling you both this in the strictest confidence, and it must not go any further than between us."

"I'll do whatever I can." She agreed. "This is my home."

"Yes, sir." Ryder nodded.

"I will be vowing our commitment to Tabitha and the Alaskan Tigers. Once I do that, I'll inform the clan and Tabitha will send some support to assist us. Guards to begin training the selected to secure our compound. Our enemies will see our supporters and will back off."

"You're doing this just to keep the clan free of others who wish to overtake you and make the clan their own?" Heidi questioned.

"You already know that my sister, Mira, is a supporter. It's why everything happened as it did." He paused for a moment, remembering pushing her toward the door and begging her to run. There had been no doubt in his mind that if Frank got his hands on her, she'd have been killed. David wouldn't risk her, but he didn't realize getting her out of harm's way would cost him so much personally, or have such an impact on the whole clan.

"Finding out she supported bringing a better future to our kind was the final break in Frank's sanity." Ryder shook his head. "It was only a matter of time, but I'm surprised it didn't happen sooner."

"He was becoming more paranoid by the day. Members were brought in for questioning because he felt like they were turning against him. He tort—" David stopped himself before he finished the word *torture* and glanced at Heidi. Brad had been one of the people Frank thought had begun to turn against, and the day before his death, he'd been tortured with the hope that he'd reveal whatever information Frank was looking for.

"You don't have to censor yourself. I know." She wrapped her arms around herself. "Brad was a good man. He tried to shelter me from what was happening within the clan, but when he was brought back to our room, there was no hiding what had happened. I doctored his wounds the best I could. I think that was the first time I realized how dangerous things were getting. I begged him to let us leave before something worse happened."

"He told me, but leaving would have signed your death warrant. Frank would've had you killed."

"Styx…" She swallowed and regained her composure. "He'd have come after us just like we'd been warned."

"That's another thing." He glanced to the end table where a family photo was displayed, the last one of them all together. Instead of looking at the false smiles spread across their faces, his gaze was on Mira. "Styx isn't the assassin he once was. He's now a guard for the Alaskan Tigers' Elders…and Mira's mate."

"You can't be serious." Shocked, Ryder leaned forward. "What, now he's killing for the opposing side?"

"Killing isn't the right word." David chose his words carefully. There was no doubt that Styx would kill someone in the line of duty or to protect those he cared about, but he was no longer the paid assassin he had been. "He's the second in the Lieutenant's mate's guards. Styx is no longer an assassin. That is another thing we will have to help the clan to adjust to, because eventually Mira will visit and her mate will no doubt escort her."

"After years of everyone being brainwashed to believe he would come after them, that might be more of a struggle to overcome than the clan accepting your commitment to the Alaskan Tigers." Heidi looked between the two before her gaze settled on Ryder. "You've been here your whole life. What do you think? The threat of Styx was never used against me by my former Alpha."

"She's right," Ryder agreed before David could answer her question. "It's hard to believe someone who's had such a career as an assassin would ever settle down to be a second in the Elder guards. He'd have to report to the Captain, the Lieutenant, and the Alpha. It's too much hierarchy for someone with his past."

"Be that as it may be, it's still the truth. I've spoken with him myself, and with his Elders. He's a changed man." David glanced back at the family photo. "Maybe Mira can help convince those who have doubts. As his mate, she'd know the truth, and she was always well liked within the clan."

"Sounds like there are going to be many battles ahead." Heidi twisted her wedding ring. "Brad would have loved to be a part of the changes, to see the clan rise above Frank's control."

"He's a part of this through us. He'll never be forgotten, and there's no better way to honor his memory than with you helping the clan through this difficult time," David reassured her.

Brad wasn't the only one who would have enjoyed seeing the clan move out of the shadows and into the sunlight. He'd have been leading the pack if he was here, making sure everyone was adjusting well. Without him, David hoped he'd be able to manage the job. The cost to overpower Frank had been great, and he'd make sure no one had died in vain. Whether they had been a supporter of Frank's or against him, none of that mattered now. The new clan would be united in the memory of those who were no longer with them.

For Shelly and Brad.

Marissa Dobson

Born and raised in the Pittsburgh, Pennsylvania area, Marissa Dobson now resides about an hour from Washington, D.C. She's a lady who likes to keep busy, and is always busy doing something. With two different college degrees, she believes you're never done learning.

Being the first daughter to an avid reader, this gave her the advantage of learning to read at a young age. Since learning to read she has always had her nose in a book. It wasn't until she was a teenager that she started writing down the stories she came up with.

Marissa is blessed with a wonderful supportive husband, Thomas. He's her other half and allows her to stay home and pursue her writing. He puts up with all her quirks and listens to her brainstorm in the middle of the night.

Her writing buddy Pup Cameron, a cocker spaniel, is always around to listen to her bounce ideas off him. He might not be able to answer, but he's helpful in his own ways.

She loves to hear from readers so send her an email at marissa@marissadobson.com or visit her online at http://www.marissadobson.com.

Other Books by Marissa Dobson

Alaskan Tigers:

Tiger Time

The Tiger's Heart

Tigress for Two

Night with a Tiger

Trusting a Tiger

Alaskan Tigers Box Set Vol. 1

Jinx's Mate

Two for Protection

Bearing Secrets

Tiger Tracks

Healing the Clan

Alaskan Tigers Box Set Vol. 2

Her Black Tiger

Tiger Trouble

Alpha Claimed

Forever Creek Shifters:

Forever's Fight

Protecting Forever

Stormkin:

Storm Queen

Crimson Hollow:

Romancing the Fox

Loving the Bears

A Lion's Chance

Swift Move

Purrable Lion

Bearly Alive

Saved by a Lion

Furever Mated Box Set

Reaper:

A Touch of Death

SEALed for You:

Ace in the Hole

Explosive Passion

Operation Family

Marine for You:

Lucky Chance

Back from Hell

A Marine's Second Chance

Tanner Cycles:

Until Sydney

Phantom Security:

Different Sides

Undercover Agent

Cedar Grove Medical:

Hope's Toy Chest

Destiny's Wish

Leena's Dream

Fate:

Snowy Fate

Sarah's Fate

Mason's Fate

As Fate Would Have It

Half Moon Harbor Resort:

Learning to Live

Learning What Love Is

Her Cowboy's Heart

Half Moon Harbor Resort Vol. 1

United Homefront Ranch:

Destination Forever

Beyond Monogamy:

Theirs to Treasure

Clearwater:

Winterbloom

Unexpected Forever

Losing to Win

Christmas Countdown

The Surrogate

Clearwater Romance Volume One

Small Town Doctor

Stand Alone:

Through Smoke

SEALed Rescue

SEALed in Texas

Starting Over

Secret Valentine

Restoring Love

www.ingramcontent.com/pod-product-compliance
Lightning Source LLC
Chambersburg PA
CBHW030616130626
46552CB00002B/589